BIG HILLS

A Western Novel
by
David Lloyd Sutton

Nothing like a good piece of hickory." - Clint Eastwood as the Preacher in Pale Rider. Ray Bradbury suggests that writing with zest and gusto is the only writing worth doing. Author David Lloyd Sutton clearly had both gripped firmly in hand when he wrote Big Hills. The scene when young Anson Kerrigan first comes to town to barter with his hard-earned goods is, alone, worth the price of admission. A unique encounter with a bear will make you wince, shout out your favorite expletive, and laugh. Fabulous action sequences, exquisite detail, a compelling story, and a protagonist to heartily root for, Big Hills packs a lasting punch. **Adam Russ**, Author of Bloodhound in Blue.

Big Hills a beautifully told tale, David Sutton has done an outstanding job of recreating the old west. His story is full of gritty realism and well-researched details of daily life on the frontier. His descriptions of the landscape of New Mexico are vivid and evocative - you feel like you are there. His characters are easy to like, the plot full of adventure, and the conclusion is just what you would like it to be. **K.E. Montieth, Author of Fiddler's Ridge.**

This is one of the best westerns I've ever read. Actually, even if you don't like westerns as a genre, you'll still enjoy the precision and beauty of the writing, as well as the action and engaging characters. Fans of the movie Open Range will appreciate this gem of a novel. **Scott Evans, Author**

I was born in south central New Mexico. I spent many long, hot hours in the desert with my grandfather as he taught me how to track. During those times he told me stories of the Old West and the men and women who struggled to settle the land. As he got older and his mind slipped the stories really came to life as grandpa thought he actually was one of the characters in his stories - and I believed him. I read David's words but I heard my grandfather's voice. It felt so real, like an actual account handed down through generations. The only negative thing about the book - it ended too soon. Thanks for the memories! ~ **Deborah Juckes, Author**

To Christina

and

Ready Flame

A six-legged, beautiful, redheaded combo; essential
to my starting this novel.

Thanks also to Professor Scott Evans and his
Blue Moon writers' group, especially to Adam Russ,
Kate Monteith, Lisa Slabach, and Ron Lane, for
their professional readings and encouragement. Ron
Lane also guided me through this publication.

The bugling, recumbent elk on the cover was
captured by a fine wildlife photographer, Jim Coda.

Contents

CHAPTER I

I taken time to shave that morning. I remember that, 'cause I couldn't afford the water for a week or two before. That New Mexico country from over around *Raton* to the center is *dry*. Even down south below that *Jornada Del Muerto*, you have sometimes a two days' ride between watering spots.

Now, *Raton* is Spanish for "Rat," and *Jornada Del Muerto* means "Route of the Dead Man." Gives you some flavor of the country. Seemed like all that lived there was antelopes and jackrabbits, and there wasn't much to choose between them for tender eating, neither.

Well, I had plenty of water now, and I'd shaved, and drunk my stomach full of hot water. First fire in a week, too. Filtering in from up Colorado way, I'd been too scared to light a fire or shoot a gun, those Utes being all over the place and me being alone; Utes were by no means all of one mind about white men in that time and place.

Now I was thinking venison.

I am Anson Kerrigan, and along about that time of my life I was given to serious thought over my next meal, because of how I hadn't had any of the previous dozen.

I had me a good Henry lever action, only real class in my outfit, and that gave me a chance at those antelope. I'd heard tell that if you lay down behind a ridge and waved a bit of white rag on a stick, they'd toll in close as two hundred yards, if you were lucky.

I had seen no Indian sign for a few days, so had risked fire, but now the hunger was catching up to me in a bad way. It was getting to be all I could do to stay in the saddle.

I gave no thought to those jackrabbits because all my Henry would leave of one of them was a red mist and a whimper, as they say. And there really isn't much to eat on a jackrabbit. They are all bones and strings and worms once they are grown up.

Only trouble was finding anything in my kit was white. Seemed like everything I owned was gone gray and thin except my guns and animals.

My only handgun was one of those big old Walker Colts. A good gun, if you had suspenders to hold up your pants and a strong wrist. I had the wrist, but not the suspenders. Now, the man I taken that hog leg and Henry off of had real nice clothes and big broad suspenders, but his wrists had been nowhere as strong as his mouth. I had his throat opened up and his arm tenons cut before he could burn me with a second round. Nobody said anything when I taken his pistol and gun belt, and shucked that Henry out of his saddle sheath and the bandolier off his saddle horn. I would have taken the rest of his outfit, too, but there appeared to be a lot of people on that small-town Ohio street who'd known him, and they all knew me, and where we lived. Even though he'd set out to humiliate and scare me, and I was clearly in the right, weapons are one thing, but beyond that folks feel different. I left that town soon after, anyway.

Mule had been Ma's, left me when the pneumonia took her off. With the guns, I was able to get meat for her those last months, but we'd been so long on so little she hadn't any strength left. I think when she'd realized Pa wasn't going to come home, the will to live went out of her.

Along about the time Ma died that big-mouthed fella's friends had started talking up a lynching, and I left out of there with what I could put together real quick. The cabin and little three-acre field bought the green-broke horse and the old saddle. There hadn't been anything else would fetch any money or was good for quick barter. I left the plow, and I had to leave the big iron cauldron, valuable as that was. They were too much to pack.

That cauldron'd made soap and boiled laundry and rendered lard and dipped hogs and heated baths, and it purely hurt to leave it, because it was all the civilization and luxury we'd ever owned.

You understand, it's one thing to fight when you have no choice but to crawl or die, but when they can come against you in the dark, and there are a lot of them, and most of them have been to war, and you are just turned fifteen, it is simple prudence to emigrate out of that place.

That had been more than two years ago, now. I had covered a lot of trails since, and worked here and there for staples and ammo, run a few times and fought a couple times too, when I couldn't run or couldn't stomach running. I hadn't killed anyone else, though. I only done it that one time because I had no way out.

It was the feel of my almost-smooth face that called to mind Ma's one other treasure...*her* mother's little silver-mounted mirror, with Ma's white lace shawl wrapped close around it, that I kept in her quilt. There was seldom call to take them out, even for shaving. At seventeen and a half a man don't need to shave all that often or all that careful. I would have buried Ma in her shawl if I'd thought of it, but I was too flat-out bawling to think about it till it was too late. I dug into Mule's load.

I looked into the mirror a bit, feelin' like I might see Ma there, but what I saw was a thin, green-eyed face, hollow in the cheeks, and with a straight nose, a sort of square chin, all tanned leather dark. My hair was blond, real long, and the sun had turned it white here and there. It was a hungry man's face, I tell you true.

The antelope came in, curious about the white waving thing, and I dropped a buck clean. But I was careful to wrap Ma's shawl and mirror in her quilt again and to roll them all snug in a piece of tarp before I started down the ridge to butcher.

CHAPTER II

The Mexican folk who came north into New Mexico were the kind of *Hidalgos* who had followers, almost family serfs, like the old English did or the Rooshians do now. So big hunks of country belonged to single families, but there were plenty of poor folk, too, long on the *Indio* blood, and sometimes all they seemed to have to get by on were the *ristras* of chili peppers hanging on their porches.

All the same, if you hailed one of those little houses, they'd feed you, every time. Even if you looked as hardscrabble and raw as I did along about then. Other travelers had told me that, like they'd told me of the routes between watering places. Those days, most information about roads and routes was word of mouth, often shared across campfires.

Early next day after I dropped that antelope buck, I helloed at a little square mud house down at the end of a long valley.

I had known it was settled country long before I sighted the smoke from the stack of that little house, because the grazing was thin, and the soil mostly bare. One thing the Texans I'd met up Kansas way had told me, none of these New Mexico folks had ever thinned down their herds, maybe because they hadn't any place to sell beef critters. Over in California they'd slaughtered for hides and tallow for years, because they could ship those things to Mexico, but in New Mexico, they had no coast, of course, and nowhere in driving range wanted for beef. Those Texans had said they were turning the whole place into a desert. Looked to me like they hadn't had a long ways to go in the first place, but that was what I'd been told.

The man who came out had empty hands, but I noticed he stayed next the door, set to duck in. There'd be a gun there. Apaches rode here, and Navaho had recent stolen cattle and horses over a big bunch of country, until General Carson stopped them. Any house away out here would have a gun.

"*Tejano*?" It wasn't a friendly question.

I smiled. "No, sir, I'm from Ohio."

"*Vaya a comer* " … and seeing how blank I must have looked, because I had about five Spanish words to my name when I first came into New Mexico, and those had been re-branded by Texans, "You come eat." He still didn't sound noways friendly, but I could smell beans, and my stomach took to rumbling. Man does not live by venison alone. Not unless he has to.

"I do thank you."

I got down and loosened up Red's cinch and took a quarter of antelope off Mule's load, and laid it down on the porch respectful. There was a post there for hitching and I went to tie up, but the man looked at me kind of thoughtful and said, "There is water … there. And a" … he gestured, "a…corral." He was showing me out back.

Sure enough there was a trough out there and a corral with a skinny little horse in it. So I watered my beasts, and put them in the corral without their tack. Then I washed my hands and face and slicked my hair back, and used one of the little knives and cleaned my nails real quick. Ma always wanted men to come clean to her table, and the habit stuck. Maybe I'd get invited to sleep inside; didn't know if I wanted to. It had been about eight months since I had slept under a roof, and that had been a feed shed in Kentucky, where I helped with some haying.

The man had a wife, which caused me delight, because the food would be woman-cooked, and a pretty little girl and two little boys. I noticed my hunk of antelope hanging from one of the log rafters, what they call *vigas*, that supported the low flat roof. It had some pieces cut off already, and the little 'uns had slices of browned meat clutched in their hands and their mouths were greasy…and grinning. Made me feel good to provide for children. After Pa got took off for the war, we had meat mighty seldom, Ma and me. Nothing to shoot with, and just what I could trap or catch, catfish and possums and such. The Cherokee boys showed me how to use a bow, and how to tan hides. It is purely hard on a boy to grow up without a man to teach him. Pa taught me some things, like how to sharpen blades and how to grow corn. But he was gone before I was come to the age of reason, and there was a lot to learn that I'd had to teach myself. I always suspected there was much more I'd never managed to learn, and it made me cautious when I was a youngster.

They gave me beans with peppers in them, and *posole,* a gruel of cornmeal with flavoring of green chilies, and even some canvasy rounds of bread they call *tortillas* thereabouts.

A fella told me once that when those Spanish conquerors, those *conquistadores*, came to Mexico, they saw the folks there made these little flat cakes of corn flour, and the Spanish only had one word for a food that looked like that. "Tortilla" means "omelette", or anyhow, it used to.

It was all fine after so long on so little, and that mostly barely seared meat, and even snake. The only thing meaner and faster than one of them rattlers is a hungry boy, I tell you true.

I slept out after all, though they offered me a place by the fire. Didn't seem proper with a woman in the house, and only one room and all. In the morning, one of the little boys came and gestured me to come in and I came and they gave me another tortilla and some beans.

Well, when I tacked up it seemed just natural to leave another ham from that antelope. His name was *Ausevio*, The man of the house, I mean, not the antelope, and hers, seems to me like every other woman and girl in New Mexico, was *Maria*. They were nice folks, and I left their house feeling a lot better about the world and with good advice about travel.

CHAPTER III

I needed to stop and make up my outfit some. This was spring, warming and green, but summer and winter would come, surely, and I had neither hat nor coat, no food but a forequarter of antelope, and only ten rounds...nine, now, for the Henry and maybe fifty for the Colt. And I needed to figure out what I was going to do. Not just this year, but I had to grow me a plan.

Four days later I was down near Las Cruces, and as night was closin' in I come up on a half dozen Anglo cowboys, camped by a little puddle they called a lake thereabouts.

"Hello the fire!" Heads turned, and a couple faded back into the dark, judicious-like.

"Light n' set, you be peaceful." The voice was calm, but the words was sincere sounding.

"Altogether peaceful. Thankee." It would have been plumb suicide to say elsewise, because I knew those fellas had faded from the fire would have me in their sights.

I unsaddled Red and Mule and put hobbles on Red. Mule would stay with him, and in any case would come to call. Red sometimes liked to wander about, nights, which could be aggravatin' on cold and rainy mornings. I tossed a tarp over my gear and put some rocks on that, as the wind was picking up speed, and moreover, picking up sand and bits of gravel as it traveled. Seemed like the wind in New Mexico always carried baggage. I took the Henry with me to the fire. They had two, actually, one big one for warmth and a bed of deep coals off to one side, obvious for cookin' on.

Those cowboys were all moppin' enameled plates with biscuits and I saw the Dutch oven off to one side had probable baked 'em. The man had returned my hail was squattin' next the cookin' fire, a bandanna around his head, and he grinned up at me from under a big mustache, dug his knife into a can, flipped a dollop of lard into a big spider-legged skillet was in the edge of the coals. "Set yourself down. We need some help here." He knifed a slab of beef off a pile that lay on a raw hide. Seeing my hungry grin, he flopped the meat into the pan, where it mostly filled the whole thing. "We put a broke-leg steer outen its' mizry. Meat won't keep and these boys just won't eat enough to do any good atall." There were a few stuffed-soundin' chuckles around the fire.

"I thank you. Been a long time since I tasted beef."

Acrost the fire there squatted a hard-faced youngster in torn shirt and shiny-rubbed leather chaps. He had him a scar through the right side of his upper lip made him snarl permanent like, and his face was bristly in patches. He wore one of them big Texas hats, and he had a bone-gripped peacemaker slung low on his right side, held in by a thong under the hammer, so's when he cocked it, drawing, it would come free. I took note of that, and have used that trick myself for many a year now. I noticed too that he wore a little bird-handled revolver high up, in front of his left hip, for cross draw. On top of that, the leather thong went roun' his throat was tight, which meant he had a throwin' knife hangin' down back of his neck. All the weaponry looked to be part of him.

"You got you one 'a them 'spensive Yankee rifles, I see, an' that Walker looks used. You ever use 'em in a *fight*?" I hadn't been the only one takin' inventory, seemed like.

It was the kinda challenge you expected 'mongst young men. Nonetheless, the other men about the fire looked a tad annoyed. "Twasn't the best of manners to bristle at someone come to your fire.

"Only when I had to." I said it mild, but lookin' straight at him. Of course my Henry was hangin' in my left hand, and I hadn't hunkered down yet, and the footing was good. We both knew that Henry could spit before he'd get a hand *to* a pistol, let alone draw it. He held real still for a moment, doin' his judgin', then he nodded and grinned his ownself. I noticed one of his front teeth, under that scar, was cracked and grey. "Only time to use em."

Their beans were nowhere as good as Maria's, but I flat-out surrounded a couple of beefsteaks. They chuckled some, but one of them had just bought a new pistol that used brass cartridges, and he gave me some powder and caps he had, for the Walker, just because he saw I had one. They were from Lincoln County, over above Roswell. They looked leaned-out and wary, but they all had good outfits and good horses, though they weren't really any older than I was, on average. They asked me if I'd ever rode cows, and I had to admit that the closest I had ever come was driving a milk cow to graze along the road when I was a tad. They seemed to understand my attitude towards fightin'. I think they were part of that upset that turned into a range war a few years after that, but they were polite and kind to me. Cowboys, by 'n large those days, was just unskilled labor on horseback. This bunch looked a cut above that; not casual drovers, but cattle handlin' professionals, with weapons skills. They called the slightly older fella had first spoke to me "Cookie", respectful, and they had a mule with panniers dedicated to carryin' cookin' gear like that skillet, the big iron Dutch oven, their bailed bean pot, and food. This was a real outfit.

My Mule carried an old fry pan and a pot, some tarps and rope, a shovel, an axe, a big bucksaw, two thin old blankets, and that fine quilt my Ma had kept from when she was a girl. I didn't use that, I just kept it rolled up tight and aired it out sometimes on sunny days. A gunnysack carried fixing tools of Pa's and a basket of Ma's tools. There was an oiled leather sack that had held beans and one that'd held parched corn, both empty for weeks now. My outfit was kinda hollow just then. The pack saddle and pa's leather-working and handy tools were all we'd had to work with all the time I was growing up and I couldn't leave them, nor could I leave Ma's sewing things, though I had to leave the dress dummy Pa had made for her before I was born. The tarps came off some abandoned wagons I found on the trail going through Kentucky. Bandits killed some poor movers, probably. Still, I needed the canvas and there hadn't been anyone to care. Now, see'in the real utility of the personal gear and outfit around me made me feel like I was packin' trash. Still, it was all I had, and I kept the rain off'n it.

I lay my blankets down out some from the fire, and when we all got up in the dawn light, that Cookie made a lot of steaks sizzle direct on coals, so everyone got to juggle hot meat as they gnawed. It was maybe more delicious than done civilized in a skillet.

Those cowboys there and in Texas call their ropes "lariats", and sometimes they call themselves "Buckaroos." Some time later, when I had learned a bit of Spanish, it came to me that "lariat" was Texas re-branding for *la riata*, the rope, and Buckaroo for *Vaquero*, cow-puncher. It's not just livestock that drifts across boundaries.

Now, not every traveler was hospitable like that. Two days northing travel, after parting from that friendly outfit, and I was in sight of some almighty big hills, and down to my last bit of that antelope shoulder.

I was crouched over my little fire, nursin' the coals under my pot that held a soup of venison and a few leaves of button sage. I'd set camp just after a little bend in the trail, ahint a big rock, out of the wind for sake of my fire. I'd expected a quiet night, but then, shod hooves clipping rock real close by gave me just a few seconds of warning that I had company.

"Hey the fire!" The foremost of two mounted figures shouted, though 'twas altogether unnecessary, him being just a couple yards away and all.

He didn't hesitate polite-like; just swung down without ary pause for my answer, as was polite at a campsite.

I put my old brass poker down in the coals. It was a silly thing to pack around, but it had been part of every fire-tending, all of my life, and I had been using it at every warm camp since I left home. I felt like I might need to have something more authoritative in my hand. This fella sounded angry.

There were just the two of them; but the other one, a lean, bird-moving man in worn blue jeans and shield shirt, was a bit less brash. He nodded, squatted down, said, "obliged," stretched thin hands to the fire.

"What'cha doin' here, Ranny?" The first and bigger one spread his feet apart right in front of me, moccasined toes almost in my fire, fists on his hips, belly sagging out. He was in old, tattery buckskins with a cap made from a coyote pelt, empty-eyed face forward, and knife handles and pistol grips stuck out all over him. He dropped a hand to brush one pistol, projectin' from near his knee.

I answered him calm and quiet, 'cause Ma always said a soft answer turneth away wrath, and this fella was wrathful if I ever met someone who was. "Just passin' through…"

He wasn't going to let it go, barked, "Passin' *our* range, Ranny? That our beef?" I caught a whiff of his breath...foul tobacco, rotten teeth, and whiskey.

His toe tipped my pot over, and the little tad o' food sizzled and spat in the coals. I felt my empty stomach clench.

I looked up at him and smiled. It seemed to take him back some. "No, that was my own venison. Is that your foot?" I made it cheerful, and he looked down, puzzled, as I sank the red-rosy poker through the top of his moccasin, into his foot, then yanked it sideways like a pry bar.

His scream was really short before I brought the poker out and around to the top of his gun wrist. Then it sorta croaked out. I stood, stepping out sideways so he was between his partner and me, clearing the Walker, and asked the Segundo, "Want some?"

He hadn't moved out of his squat, had his hands still out to the fire, open and empty, and now he just shook his head. "Nossir. I'm just in the wrong place tonight."

His big friend was down, holding his stab-burned foot and kinda keening.

"That's pretty clear. Any food in his bags?"

He was some took back, but answered prompt-like, "Yessir...bacon and cornmeal and such..."

"Put alla your weapons in a pile here by the fire, real slow, and then put that food alongside them."

I left their weapons on their tied horses, a mile from where I'd had my fire, so's they'd be able to find 'em. I suspected that little man would be the one trailin', 'cause his smelly friend wasn't going to be an enthusiastic walker for a time.

I settled in a good five miles further on, in a defensible position. But I toasted bacon over a new fire and roasted corn dodgers on a hot rock. The old poker mended my new fire too.

After that night I was more careful, setting my camps in places where getting up on me was more problem than before.

Mountains in New Mexico don't mean trees and streams and game like they do some places. At least, not *all* the mountains. Still, I headed up high in the *Sierra Blancas* after just skirting North of Las Cruces.

Coming from where I had, and the way I had, I'd seen mountains far off up in Colorado...the *Sangre De Christos*... the Blood of Christ Mountains, but these here White Mountains were the biggest hills I'd ever actually ridden into.

I taken a few days in the foothills, where there was water and shade, to kill a deer and eat my fill a while. I was thinkin' on my outfit.

My pants had been good homespun wool once, and I had me a stout piece of bull hide for a belt…no buckle, but I was used to tying the cinch knot. For a shirt I had buckskin, gone shiny and greasy here and there, but it kept the wind out. Still, I had me both short and long guns, a good belt knife and a couple of short fine ones, and a razor that had been one my Pa left when he taken out for the war. My big red horse was trusty and steady by then. He'd been so green when I got him that I'd spent half of my traveling time chasing him whilst nursing bruises from hitting the ground. His saddle still had a good tree and a sound cinch, but the leather was just hanging on from habit. I figured I needed to upgrade some to get to decent. Maybe the means were above me here, in the high country.

A jackrabbit lived close in to my camp, had him a cottontail friend. I'd come on 'em, big hare sittin' and watchin' one way, little rabbit behind him, about three feet away, watching t'other direction. Both were males, different species, but partnered for security. Red and Mule and me were like that, some, but our partnership wasn't altogether voluntary, like that Jack and that bunny. They were together like that every afternoon we stayed in that low camp. I figured they added a lot to each other's survival.

Days of riding took me ever higher, and the forest became tall and green, with soft things growin' low, all spread over long canyons that angled up to become green tunnels into the sky.

The ravens began to have a sound to their flight, *Whiiiuuu, whiiiuuu,* and then a long hiss as they planed down. I'd never thought the sound of birds flying would change up high, but it did.

I had no money to use in a town, and would have to put together my outfit from the land. These past two years I had been moving through Kentucky and Missouri and Kansas, and I have to tell you, where people have settled in, it's hard to take from the land. They feel they own it all, you see, and they guard it, even if it ain't properly theirs. If you don't belong, they push on you. That first winter, in Missouri, I had spent my time wrapped up in tarps and huddled over fires, and for the worst part of it, I put a tarp over an old pigpen stockade I found, clean-smelling from being empty for years, but along about February a mean little man with a shotgun called me a trespasser, and he laid claim to the whitetail I had hanging from a black locust, too. I was shivering too hard to argue, so Red and Mule and me taken out. Lucky enough that day was the first real sunshine in weeks.

Sure enough, we went through junipers, and then *piñons*, and then into the big Douglas Firs and Ponderosas. We were up maybe nine thousand feet, and Red got winded on short hills and I got winded on short walks and Mule was just flat winded. I had been seeing the gnawed alder bark that Ausevio had told me showed elk winter-feeding ever since I'd gotten above the little *piñons*. He'd told me about pine nuts, too, but it was too early. I didn't want to use the Henry if I could help it, so I needed to leave the animals and still-hunt, to get close enough for pistol-shot.

With the bucksaw and shovel and axe, I built a tight corral and set sharpened stakes all around the outside to at least slow down bears and wolves. If I lost my mount and my pack animal I might not make it out to the low country again. Then I took a whole day to build a lodge of fallen logs and dirt, about ten feet long and five wide, maybe four foot high at the peak, so I would have somewhere to shelter if a late snowstorm came in. My blankets were thin, and I had no fat on me at all. I made a little shelter outside the lodge for a fire, piled wood and stone, made a wood-pliers with branches and thongs so I could bring in heated rocks from the outside fire. I cut boughs to make a door that would cut the wind some.

I don't mind telling you, I was some scared. Ohio was settled country. People were always within a few miles, at least, and while I was used to being alone and leaning on my own gitup to live, this was high-up alone, and there wasn't even a distant whiff of wood smoke or a hoof print in a week's travel.

I needed clothes, and a good coat, maybe a robe or two, a lot of food I could carry out, new foot gear, and probably new tack for my animals. That meant a lot of hides, and a lot of work.

Before I killed anything, I needed to be ready to take care of it. So I set up sort of a teepee of fir boughs over a big rack of branches. Jerky is hard to do without salt, but the trick is to let the smoke work in and turn the meat, cut real thin, tasty and cured and dry. The fir boughs would slow the smoke down, but wouldn't let the heat build up. If you get the meat too hot it cooks instead of curing, and then it spoils as sure as the sun comes up in the morning. We used to say you could worry off a hunk of good jerky and have chewing for the whole day. If you want to do big hunks of meat, then you have to have salt to get the first juices out, the way farmers do country hams. Without any salt I had no choice but to make jerky.

A couple miles back I'd come up a hillside covered with little oak trees like chest-high bushes, thick as could be. I would use oak to make my smoke. Pine and fir and juniper are all unsuitable for smoking meat. I taken Mule back there and an hour with the axe loaded him down good enough. I had to give Mule time to get used to the altitude. He was older than me, after all.

CHAPTER IV

There were at least twenty cow elk in the meadow below me, but the closest was a good seventy yards off. I needed to be closer, to use the Walker. It taken me an honest hour to work out into the meadow, moving low, like a snake, and after the first couple of feet, I was drenched with icy water from the low grasses and mosses. The elk droppings stained me up some, too.

Finally, I was close enough I could hear them breathe. I tell you true, that was inspiring. They were the biggest deer critters I had ever seen till then. I taken one shot each, and I shot for the vitals, just behind the upper foreleg. I shot into three of them before the herd crashed off into the forest. I was standing in a cloud of gun smoke, and my ears were ringing.

Only one target went down where I could see her, blowing pink froth into the air, and trying hard as she could to get up and run.

It made me hurt to see her hurt, but I couldn't afford to shoot any more if I didn't have to. I ran in quick, and laid her throat open as neat and deep as I could with my belt knife, and then taken off on the other blood trails. One got almost a half mile before she folded, but she was all the way dead when I got there. Only, after I found the last one, I realized I'd been carrying that Walker at full cock, at a dead run through broken ground. It settled me down some, and I was real careful uncocking and putting the hammer down on an empty nipple. I was heaving and blowing so hard I almost fell down with dizzy. All that excitement had made me forget there wasn't much air to be had up there.

Long after dark, I finished dressing out the first one, and got the hide clean off. Still, I went all the way back to Red and Mule, almost two miles, with a hunk of elk the size of my leg, and the hide, before I kindled fire and ate. Then I took the Walker apart real careful on canvas, and boiled water to clean the empty cylinders and barrel, because that black powder would eat the metal if I didn't. I loaded it up, and left a cap off the nipple of one cylinder for the hammer to ride, like always.

Mule didn't like carrying fresh blood, but we'd worked this out back in Ohio when I was a lot younger, and even Red carried his share of elk next morning. Still, it took me two days to get all the meat and hides into camp, and I made charitable contributions to some wolves and coyotes without really meaning to.

After that, I had to tend the smoke fire, watch my animals on tethers where they grazed, and spend an awful lot of messy hours scraping big hides.

All the time, I was kind of dreading and kind of hoping all that meat and blood smell would attract a bear, because I would need bearskins too. No bears came then, and I used brains and livers and even my own pee for tanning, after I soaked the hides in a little stream and scraped out the hair.

Elk skin leather stays soft even after it gets wet. But back in Ohio, we had big oak trees to give us bark for tanning, and here all I had was thin-skinned oak bushes and smelly things that I'd never tried serious before. This brains-and-liver-paste trick was something the Cherokee boys had showed me, but I'd always used oak bark to cure my rawhide, given a choice, 'cause of the stink of that other way. Still, a week after I fired the first shot, I tugged the drying hide of an elk to stretch and limber it, pounded the first length of dried tenon to free sinew for sewing, and started a new pair of trousers. My old homespuns were two inches above the tops of my wore-out boots, and they were no longer socially acceptable, having been rubbing against a saddle long enough there wasn't much of anything left to cover my sit-down.

I don't think I've ever worked as hard as I did that spring. But by full summer, I had new boots, with shafts to my knees, tall moccasins, two pair of elk-skin trousers with shoulder straps and thong-laced side flaps, so they fitted tight under my belts and wouldn't come down, running or riding, and double thick inside my legs and on my seat, two mid-thigh elkskin shirts, and a full-length coat with a big split skirt to let me wear it riding. I patterned that after those dusters riders wore then, but it was some heavier, for true. The only thing I couldn't figure out how to make was a hat. What with mule deer and so on, I had saddlebags, and new sheathes for all of my knives, and I had about twice Red's weight of smoked jerky. Why, I even stitched up a slicker out of strips of slit, flattened elk intestine, oiled and as good as anything a general store ever carried. I made a lot of sacks of that, too, to keep jerky and dried berries and rendered fat. Ma made dresses for other ladies, to get us some money for flour and salt and such, and winters, without any coats, we were inside a lot. I had learned to sew good.

It was a lot of careful work making elk-skin head stalls, and replacing parts of my saddle. I had a few steel needles amongst my gear, but they were altogether too small to sew sinew with. I had to make needles out of bone, and then after a couple of days working on bone needles I found shaved yucca thorns were better; using a loop of some attached fibers to pull the sinew through allowed the holes in the leather to be a lot smaller than what was required to pass a needle with an eye big enough for sinew.

Finally, I had to figure out something would be good to trade for money for cartridges for the Henry, lead, caps, and powder for the Walker. I needed a good stone for my razor, some flour, and some kind of hat.

Most days I worked near naked, half of the time, covered in blood and grease, putting my new things aside careful as I got them made. Nights I had the fire, and meat spitting, broth boiling. Mule and Red plumped up nice on that high country bunch grass once they got used to the thin air.

There was scraping and tanning work to do every day, and every night I sat close to my banked coals and braided horsehair, made twine of yucca, and stitched on small work.

Every morning I cast out wide, just looking and smelling and listening. There was no sign of men, and I felt a lot of tight-necked tension go away over the long weeks.

Sometimes I took a few hours and just lay out, sunning and sleeping. Other days I took Red, with mule ponying loose along, and gathered onions and berries and cattail roots and oak wood. All in all, I felt good about the world. A full belly and warm camps can do that. I missed people less every day.

Whenever I killed an elk or a deer I ate liver, all I could hold, which is a lot, and I cleaned kidneys to toast too, because the organ meat was like cream amidst all that red meat. I really missed salt, but wood ash helped a bit.

One late afternoon I was layin' in the lodge, door off to one side, because while warm it was drizzlin' some outside, and slicin' off pieces of smoked meat to gnaw on. All of a sudden, the light from my doorway went out, and there was a "WHUFF" and a "WHACK" of really big teeth slamming together. I had me a bear visitor at last, and I was in a one-door place too short to even stand up in. My Henry was out with my saddle, in its boot, under a tarp to keep off the wet. The Walker was layin' alongside me, had only four cylinders full, me havin' used it recent, and not had time to clean it yet. I come up in a squat, dropping my knife as I grabbed the Walker, and leveled that heavy thing two-handed, eared back the hammer, and the bear lunged further in, just total pluggin' off the light, and so I poked the muzzle out 'till I felt it touch somethin' boney, and fired. The muzzle blast lit up the bear's face, so I saw I had shot just alongside the fringes of its muzzle, tearin' loose a flap of side lip left a lot of big teeth bare, and the stink of singed hair and the roar came together, so's I just cocked and fired again, movin' the muzzle to where I thought was center. This time the flash showed me I had fired near between the critter's eyes, a bit high, and bone was showin' along the trench that ball had torn all the way up the big skull. The burned hair made smoke, choked me up some. I seen from the shape of its face that my visitor was a Grizzly, which did nothin' to comfort me. The bear recoiled just a bit from this hit, and so there was a squirt of light from underneath the big chest. I put my muzzle into its left eye, pokin' it in hard, and dropped hammer the third time. Same time I fired, somethin' really heavy hit my leg just acrost the knee, the Walker and I parted company, and I bounced hard off the inside wall of the lodge. It was rough mud on tree limbs, and it took the skin off my arm like a wood rasp takes wood. It was quiet, altogether, which was no reassurance atall, me bein' deaf from the Walker firin' in a closed place like that, and the roarin', and I held real still, but no jaws closed on me, and after a long time I felt about and found my knife, and then, after what seemed like forever, the Walker.

It was gettin' close in there, because that big beast plugged the door end of my little lodge all the way, and I had covered the whole thing with a couple feet of earth and mud among and over several layers of tight-woven branches. The scorched hair stink had me coughing and gasping hard. The bear was in almost to its hips, leaving me only a few feet of room, and I could not get my arm past its haunches to the air.

I hadn't any choice. I was smotherin' and the only way out was past that there bruin. Fortunate it was dead. Unfortunate, I couldn't squeeze past even a little bit, and I sure couldn't shove a thousand and a half pounds of carcass out the door.

So I started cutting. You don't ever want to have to tunnel lengthwise through a bear in the dark, but I had it to do and I done it. I went in just ahint the ribs, and made a long cut down from the spine, reached in and *scooped*. A whole buncha things went *schloop* out onto the floor of my lodge, and I realized my Walker was 'neath that gut pile, but breathin' was gettin' too scarce to worry about armament just then. I taken all my clothes off, and stretched into where the guts and liver had been, squirming and wriggling and hard put to breathe at all. I reached the knife in, following the big intestines, and got the point out just alongside the bung hole, and even though it smelled a lot of bear innards, that air was sweet, I tell you true. It taken me several minutes further wigglin' and cuttin' to squeeze through, but with air to breathe I could afford some patience.

Had there been anyone to see, me comin' out the bear the way I come could have made quite a story. Red and Mule was sensibly tryin' to demolish their corral in order to leave the country, and it took me some time to calm them, talking from downwind so's not to make it worse. Then, even before I moved the fire over to light a long night of skinning and butchering, I put the Henry close, and put stakes around my lodge the way I had done for the corral. I was glad of the rain, just then, havin' various bear juices in my hair and bear grease all over me. So I shivered, grateful to be able to shiver. After a bit I noticed I was limping, and saw three big grooves outside and around to the back of my right knee, where that intruder had swatted me. I was some stiff for a few days, but fortunate, once I had poured near-boilin' water to clean 'em, those claw marks didn't infect.

By the morning light I had a horse-sized pile of bear meat off to one side on some pine boughs, rain rinsin' through it to spread a big red puddle amongst the grasses and pine needles. Good thing, fat as that meat was, it wasn't leachin' the way deer or elk meat would, and with the little breeze it was gettin' chilled good. O'course, so was I, and it was becomin' hard to hold my knife, I was shakin' so hard.

The hide, with lots of attached fat, lay hair down, coverin' an area was longer than me both ways. By dawn's light I could see to scrape out my lodge, bringing out another pile, of gritty offal, uncoverin' my poor Walker. I didn't even try to toast liver, 'cause by then the smell of bear was not helping my appetite any. I cleaned the Walker, as best I could without wasting the one load was still in a cylinder, whilst stoking a big long fire in the lodge, burning up the blood and other things had soaked the floor, and heating that little room up like a kiln. The Walker had some etchin' from the blood and other things, and its bluing was mostly gone anyway. I toasted a sliver of bear fat and gave the pistol a good coat of grease. Using warm ashes, I scrubbed myself, gettin' blood and grease out of my hair, and scrubbed everything raw with charcoal, let the rain rinse me. Before I finished scraping the lodge out again, leaving a dry, warm place, I was tremblin' with tired and cold, so I just crouched in there for a bit, kinda bakin' myself, though I knew I needed to put my beasts to grazing. They had never stopped snortin' and fidgetin' all night, were sure to be hungry, and had to be tired, too.

I dozed off some there, but got dressed and put Mule and Red out, getting jerked around some and my foot stepped on as they lunged and snorted and pranced about. I hobbled Red as usual, and today hobbled Mule, too, because I wasn't sure he might not head back for Ohio, the way the place smelled. Lucky they were hungry, because grazing helped quiet them down some.

I made a drag of boughs and after I had salvaged all the inside fat I could, took the gut pile far out, figuring the coyotes would clean it up for me.

I had that huge hide to scrape clean, fast as I could, but it had chilled well and the fur was unlikely to slip right off, so I napped a few hours in my lodge oven. When I crawled out, a cloud of ravens lifted off the meat pile.

Just as well I was lame, 'cause cleaning that hide of fat and membrane cost me three days of sitting work, and I took Mule off to pick oak bushes again, scraping bark into my pot and boiling out the tannin this time.

There was no way to make jerky of meat with as much fat as that bear's had in it, so I sectioned it small as I could and smoked and cooked it down, figuring that without salt like you'd use on pork, that was the only way to keep it good for any time. I grilled ribs half as long as I was tall, and was greasy about the lips for days. My grizzly was a boar, and the flavor was strong, but still it was good, rich food, and it was good to be the one doing the eating, too.

Bear fat was good not only for lubricating weapons, but for frying, and for oiling boots.

Chewed twigs were good for tooth cleaning, using some more wood ash, and yucca fibers helped get the meat out from between my teeth. The ground down where the yuccas grew was too hard to dig well though, so I hadn't many of their roots, for either food or washing, so I used wood ashes, bear lard, and some mint juice, and, at the cost of tying up my one pot for a couple of days, came up with a kind of soap, inferior soap, 'cause my wood ashes were all from soft wood, but it worked like soap, sorta. After my spring tanning, and that trip through a bear I needed to get clean! That soft, gooey almost-soap stored good in tied-off intestine tubes too.

A few weeks after my house guest, I come on another bear, which looked argumentative, and this time I used the rifle first. It still died hard, costin' me a lot of ammo, and a good fright, and I am never goin' to pick another fight with a Grizzly as long as I live.

Now there were just two cartridges left for the Henry.

After a lot of work I had me a hooded cape or robe that went around me about twice, all of bearskin that weighed about what a bear did, live. Red and Mule got the worn old wool blankets as saddle pads. Even after I'd tanned and sewn them, those bearskins made my transport troops nervous, so I made pads of the remnants of the big hides, and sewed those into the saddle blankets, so they were a lot thicker and softer where the saddles actually sat. After a couple of days the bucking stopped, but Mule looked at me sour at saddling time for weeks.

The idea came to me whilst I was making a vest out of elk skin to give me some pockets, and to have something to wear when the air was too cold to wear just a shirt and not cold enough to wear my bearskin Storm Stopper, a garment, to be honest, I couldn't wear daytimes for more than ten breaths unless it got a lot colder than it had gotten since I had assassinated those poor bears.

I made ten of those vests. I sawed and filed discarded antlers for buttons, and drilled them with an Indian pump, a shaft of wood, a drilled plate of wood, and thongs attached to the top end of the shaft and the ends of the plate. Tiny flakes of flint or chert made drill tips. I made those vests big enough for me, and a couple big enough to make me a tent. Then I made another pair of saddlebags, a pair of moccasins that had more fringe than I'd ever seen, and a range coat of elk skin that would fit a really big man, with a collar and lapels and short cape of left-over bear skin.

By the time I got done I never wanted to sew with sinew again, and if anybody'd asked me to tan more elk skins right then, I'd have done serious violence on their person.

But I had me trading goods for the things I needed.

And I had grown me a plan.

CHAPTER V

Now, most folks who live in towns don't think much about money. Oh, they always want it, or more of it, but they don't think on just how handy it is. The thing about money is, you can divide it up, and spend some here and some there, and it doesn't weigh near as much as the things it can get you. Handy, like I said.

But I hadn't any money, so I couldn't go to the barber and get my razor sharpened, or to the saloon and buy a beer, or even pay a livery to stable my beasts for a night so I could stay in town. I had to turn some of my work into some money.

Las Cruces was a small place, and most of it was Mexican folks, which are fine folks, but they don't use money much at all, and I needed some stuff they wouldn't have in their little *tiendas*.

So I taken myself and Red and Mule to the Anglo General Store, first thing I rode in. I'd cleaned up for town, and made shift to use Ma's old hairbrush and to shave good, and to make all my gear look as good as I could. My hair was all yellow from sun, and I had tied it back neat with a thong. I tell you true, I was some proud of my new outfit, feeling happy.

So the four idlers on the long porch got a nod and a smile, as I hoisted some sacks of jerky and a couple vests off Mule's load. Mule looked like a little donkey under the packs I had on him that day!

"Ainchu the dude! Yu' som' kinda squaw man? Or justa
squaw?" Half the passerby heard him, and heads turned. I
caught a smile or two at my expense.

All of my happy went away.

He was wearing old Reb clothing and he was leaning
back against the store front just left of the door, on a three-
legged stool that didn't look too sturdy. All those other idlers
laughed real good at his remark. They had them a couple
buckets of beer, probably from the saloon across the street,
and they had obvious been drinking for some time.

Well, I could go to Deming, or to Albuquerque, both a
lot of dry riding, or I could do business here. I have thought
on it some since, and I think living on meat and fat and little
bits of wild onions and berries for those last months had put
an edge to my temper that ain't there by nature.

That man was a big 'un, and I'm not. I mean, not real big.
I weighed myself one time, and I was one hundred and sixty
pounds, and I never got as tall as six foot. But I was always
quick, and had good co-ordination. I mean, I could move.

This idler slopped over his belt some, an' his face was
kind of red, and he didn't seem to have much thickness to his
legs.

I skipped up onto that porch, and swept my boot around
like a kitten grabbing a ball of yarn. The stool came down,
and Big 'Un with it, before the sacks I'd had on my shoulder
hit the dirt. I was wearing the Walker on my left side, cross-
draw under my new coat, so when he came roaring up, I
taken a lick across the right side of his face with it, backhand.
He flopped down sudden and didn't move no more.

I just moved my foot back, and the Walker bore on those
other three hooligans natural-like. I didn't want to cock it,
because then I'd have to look at it careful to roll the cylinder
around to the empty nipple. That's how green I was then. I

thought because I had the pistol out they'd stay still. Howsomever, I have learned people who don't respect surrender themselves tend to ignore the opportunity. The two in the middle went for their belt guns, and the one on the far end reached for a falling block rifle was leaning alongside his chair.

I didn't have time to be scared; just eared back the hammer and let it fall. That rifle kind of splintered apart, the reachin' fellow reared back from the splinters and fell over, sprawlin'. When I pulled back that hammer again, I was stepping in against the wall, almost on top of Big 'Un. From there I could bear on the side of the one next in line, but he'd have to both clear leather and swivel to shoot at me, and his sidekick had a choice of shooting through him, or stepping out and around. They just crouched there with their mouths open, froze halfway to their feet, an' starting to look some worried. That Walker was a fine pistol, but it really needed to have wheels on it so's it could hang around with the other cannons. The muzzle blast and smoke and the big gout of flame from the bear lard I topped the cylinders with was some daunting, I tell you true.

"Now, why don't you gentlemen just drop those guns real easy, and we can talk about politeness to strangers?" I poked the Walker gentle-like into the ear of my nearest neighbor.

The next nearest of them lowered his hands very slow, unbuckled his belt and let the whole rig down real gentle. It occurred to me that that was a nice safe way to disarm. I smiled at the end one, who was hesitating. "Like he did, slow and easy..."

I clamped my hand on the near arm of the one I was up against, who had frozen in place when my Walker kissed his earhole, and he shucked *his* belt without any more prompting; I brought him in close to me so the Walker would fire acrost his shoulder blades. He smelt of beer and tobacco and he'd needed a bath for at least a month. I suspected his bladder was about to blow, he was shaking so hard.

I could feel myself still smiling, but I didn't feel real friendly, if you know what I mean, and I guess that end man who'd had his rifle shot to pieces took my meaning, because he shucked too, 'most as soon as he got to his feet.

I was some lucky, because they'd all had enough beer to slow them down, and not enough to ignore danger.

Folks talk about rights, and by and large, I agree that rights are a good thing. But if you want to have your rights respected, you have to respect those belongin' to other people. What I mean is, after you go to take any one of mine, I don't feel called upon to respect any of yours.

My dignity is one of my rights.

That is why I taken away their guns and belts and boots before I made those men carry their sleeping friend to the center of the street.

There was a little crowd now in front of the saloon, and I noticed people peeking out from the store's windows.

I turned to the saloon crowd. "I would appreciate directions to the Sheriff?"

The bartender was there with his white apron, which was how I knew he was the bartender, and he chuckled some, and said, " He is probably somewhere around Prescott about now, moving fast. That Rogers fellow," (he nodded at the man I had stroked with the Walker,) "called him last week and our sheriff chose to fold."

"Well, then, I guess I got no recourse. You men!" The three conscious ones and the one who was just groaning awake all startled and gaped at me.

"You have a minute to pray. If you want to kneel, I won't get flustered none."

"What ...you gonna do?" This, kind of quavery, from the last one who'd disarmed. I could see he was regretting not trying while he still had a pistol and leather on his feet.

The crowd at the saloon milled an' muttered. I ignored the idlers in the street, spoke to the crowd, keeping my voice low so they'd quiet down to hear me. That Walker just focused people's attention, somehow. I continued, "Don't worry. We're just having a prayer meeting."

I looked back at my prisoners. "Bow your heads."

"Damned ifn' I will! Yu gimme my gun back an' aih'll take thet pretty scalp of yourn, yu..." The fella who'd started the whole shebang was full awake again, though his face was swelling up something alarming. And he was obvious a poor learner.

Like I said, I suspicion that long time of no beans or bread or pie nor nothing put me in a short-tempered way.

I taken three long strides out there, and when he raised up his arm to protect his head, I broke his wrist with a quick flick of the Walker's barrel, and swatted that fella right across where I'd hit him before, being careful to get my thumb firm in front of the hammer first, so as not to fire careless or lose the cap.

He kind of screamed or maybe shrieked, and knelt down right there, with his head held in his hands, and the others all bowed their heads right nice and accompanied me in praying.

"O Lord, give us the wisdom to be polite to the stranger within our gates." I looked around..."Come along, brothers! This is a reesponsive prayer meeting here!"

There was a ragged chorus, "O Lord..."

After that I led them in a rendition of a couple of verses of "Those Who Dwell Beneath the Skies" and one of them had a good voice. A couple of the crowd over at the saloon joined in, and a really nice lady's voice from the store behind me, too.

Then I mounted Red and escorted my hobbling herd a mile out of town, deep into the *Malpais*, the nasty volcanic rock and cactuses. I didn't want to go any further into that kind of going, because my friend Red was barefoot too. They were all bloody-footed, but serious quiet. I gave them a homily. "Pray, brethren, that none of you are dumb enough to be in my sight, or my sights, for ever and ever, amen."

When I got back to the store, nobody had bothered Mule, or the weapons and boots I'd left on top of his packs, which was good for them, because I was thinking harsh thoughts, and Mule tended to kick sideways at strangers.

CHAPTER VI

I dusted off my sacks of jerky, and the vest that fell wrong, and went into that store like I'd started out to do an hour before. Behind a long counter was a man, about sixty, and an old lady looked just like him, which was a pity, because he hadn't no chin at all, and a girl.

Not just a girl; a young woman about my height or a bit more, with smooth brown hair, wearing a severe grey dress with white piping that did nothing at all to disguise just how really grown up her figure was. She had a chin, which convinced me right there she couldn't be no relative of the old folks, and her face was so pretty I stopped moving sudden-like. I got going again pretty quick. It wouldn't do at all for her to see me gawking like a calf.

I saw her lips quirk up just a tad bit. She'd noticed.

I put the sacks and vests on the counter gentle. "Sir, Ladies? I come to trade."

The old gentleman was quiet, but the old lady spoke sharp and disapproving; "This isn't a trading post, it's a store."

Well, I had some convincing to do, so I kept quiet whilst I spread out a vest and smoothed it down. I'd turned all the seams, stitched regular and neat like Ma had taught me. On both stomach pockets of this one, I'd done a pattern of crosshatched, flattened and tip-clipped porcupine quills I'd dyed with leaves and berries. Stingin' nettle gives you yellow, blackberries a good purple, and Lupine blossoms boil up a fine blue.

The girl moved over, the way a ship must move, just smooth and gliding, put out a slim hand to stroke the golden leather, ran a finger along a red quill. "This is...elegant. Your wife's work?" Her smile was about as sweet as any I'd ever seen, and I spoke slow, so as not to choke up. Just her thinking I was old enough to be married made me feel glad …and a bit scared, for some reason.

"No, ma'am, this here is my own work. I kilt the elk, and tanned the hide… and talked the porcupine out of his quills." Seems somehow I'd forgotten about girls, trying to keep alive and all. I was glad of my nice new elk skin coat.

She grinned gaily. "A tailor and a diplomat as well as a gunfighter?! You *are* a talented fellow!"

I had to grin my ownself and look down, fidgeting with the fall of that coat some, and said, apologetic, "I am sorry about that ruckus, folks. That Rogers, he said something I couldn't walk past." I felt my neck heating up some more.

The old gentleman spoke up at last. "He says something hard to take, to just about everyone, just about every day. It's time *someone* gave him comeuppance. He and his crew have been camped on my porch and insulting my customers and harassing my niece Gwendolyn here ever since he ran that useless sheriff out of town." So they *were* relatives, but it sure looked unlikely to me.

"Then happy to be of service, Sir. If you can't use the vests, could you use elk jerky?" I was feeling a bit anxious, if the truth be told. I had just made some intemperate men mad, and I hadn't but two cartridges left for the Henry, and maybe one more full load for the Walker, if I undercharged a bit.

"What do you want?" The old lady looked hard at him, and he spoke clear to her. "We have always traded for good stock from good folks. Let it be." Maybe his soul had a chin, because he sure sounded like he ran his own roost.

Upshot was, I got me a hundred rounds for the Henry, about twice as much in powder and caps and slug lead for the

Walker, plus a bullet mold in the right caliber and a ladle for melting the lead, a fine white Arkansas stone for my razor, a big lump of beeswax, two dark blue shield shirts of thick cotton, two pair of wool socks, two good heavy wool blankets and a thick canvas soogan to hold them, a twenty-pound sack of rock salt, a new rasp for hooves, some brass buckles, and, best of all, a fine felt hat in the Texas style, with a hatband and stampede cords of braided horsehair. It felt like I had my very own roof.

I traded all ten vests and about four hundred pounds of jerky. Then I looked at what I had, and at what they had, and I went out to Mule again, pulled those frilly tall moccasins out, and taken them in to add to the pile on the counter. The old folks just looked at me, and I said, "I want to give full measure." The old man smiled, like he'd just made a good point to someone, and the old lady come out when I was re-lashing my load; put a five pound bag of coffee beans in my hand. She smiled then, and you could see she'd been near pretty once. "We do too, Mr. ...?"

"Kerrigan, Ma'am. Anson Kerrigan"

"I am Imogene Dutton, and my husband is Paul. You come again, Mr. Kerrigan, you come any time."

CHAPTER VII

Half a mile away was one of those *tiendas*, and I traded a hundred and fifty pounds of jerky for ten pounds of beans, ten of cornmeal, a *ristra* of chili peppers, and a five pound bag of coarse flour. I had to use gestures, but by the time I was done, I knew the words for what I had bought, and for what I had traded.

I was all set for the trail. But I had me a problem. I didn't really want to go. I wanted to go talk to that Gwendolyn girl.

On top of that, I still didn't have any money, and stashed back up-trail a day's travel, I had another thousand pounds of jerky, and a few hundred pounds more a couple thousand feet up in the Sierra Blancas. Those hides had come off big animals, and I never could waste anything.

I managed ten miles out of town before I camped, taking care to find shelter for my fire. Red and Mule taken to grazing like beasts who hadn't eaten all day, which was the case, and I swirled sticks in a puddle in the flour sack, and toasted lump after lump of camp bread. It was *Masa Harina,* made from corn, and not wheat flour like I'd thought, but it was welcome, nonetheless.

Then I committed an error. I crushed some of those coffee beans in my pot, using my knife pommel, and boiled them in water. I'd tasted coffee once or twice in camps where I was a guest; wasn't real sure I liked it. But I drank this and chewed the lumps from my crude grinding. Result was, despite that new soogan and blankets, and being tired as all get out, the sun was coming up before I could get to sleep.

All I did all night was think of that Gwen girl. That wasn't in the plan.

I didn't try to make Mule carry his own weight in jerky. I made us a couple of travois, and let him and Red pull 'em. Red had learned a lot since Ohio, and this was another learning experience for both of us. I only had to gather up the sacks of jerky and remake Red's travois twice.

I headed past Las Cruces this time, lined out for Deming. It seemed to me I'd find someone who would pay me money for cured meat where there was a cavalry camp.

It taken me three weeks, because of having to wait at the *Rio Puerco* to ford. Story goes that that river got its name when the first Spanish man to see it said, "What a *pig* of a river!" It *was* the dirtiest water I'd come across. I had to trade a hundred pounds of my jerky for a scrawny donkey, to carry the water we had to pack. Two casks and the donkey's pack cost me another hundred pounds. Of course, I filled my casks from a well at the trading post. No one had any sense drank water from the Rio Puerco.

Outside Deming, I found a really hungry lieutenant of cavalry and two dozen troopers, who'd been living on hard tack and beans for a month. Best luck I'd had in a coon's age! I rode back for Las Cruces sixty dollars richer, because that lieutenant was a really big man and my remaining trade jacket fit him so good he paid me ten dollars for it.

Then at the Rio Puerco ford a man paid me two dollars for the saddlebags I'd made for trade.

I thought hard about selling off the donkey and tack, but considered that I might want to make a long trip again. In New Mexico that means packing water. The donkey was getting fatter, too. I figured she'd been really starved for a long time, because she went into the bunch grass south of the *Rio Puerco* like she was starving. Mule was leaned down some, and that bunch grass did him good.

Why Las Cruces, you might ask? Well, I had a few hundred pounds of jerky and some tools stashed...All right. It was because of that Gwen girl. She was playing hell with my plan.

I didn't want to use up any of my money for supplies...because it was the first real money I'd ever had...so I went north around Las Cruces again, up to my higher cache. This time I took all but a couple sacks I left for dire emergency. Whole batch was about four hundred pounds, or the yield of maybe three elk. I figured I could offer the Duttons first refusal, and dicker anyhow all over town for enough supplies to see me through to California, or at least to get me over to Nevada. One part of my plan was getting out of New Mexico to someplace not so hard-edged.

Up high, New Mexico was rich and beautiful, and even down low it was pretty, all the colors seemin' richer and more vivid than in other places, but not real attractive to a man who loved the land and green growing things. Nobody could live up in the mountains in the winter, unless they flat holed up with a ton or two of food and a small mountain of cut wood.

The way people had to live down in the towns took my heart out. Mostly it was thin soil and scarce water and the way everything seemed to be tied up.

Now, when I took those guns and boots and things from those hooligans in Las Cruces, I had stashed them up here with the rest of my jerky, hardly looking at them. After all, with the ammo the Duttons sold me, I had plenty to shoot with.

Howsomever, I was heading out, and I'd be going back to a place where I probably had enemies now, unless those idlers really taken out for safer parts, which last I doubted, human folk being so generally cussed and all.

There were three belt guns and five knives. One of the pistols caught my eye. It was the '58 New Army, .44 caliber, the way it was run up by the Confederacy, with the backstrap and trigger guard out of brass. It was in a flapped U.S. holster. Only, this *hombre* had him five pouches on his belt, held two extra cylinders, from the union version, but just as interchangeable as all get out, and he had a powder flask and a pouch of bullets and wads, and another one of caps, nestled in folds of linen.

I put flask, wads, bullets, and caps in one of my saddlebags, along with the same kind of gear for the Walker.

This was some rig for one of those trifling fellas. I was real interested in anything could give someone eighteen shots before they had to measure powder and tamp in bullets and wads and crimp on caps. Why, the second bear went into my Storm Stopper had absorbed five rounds from the Henry and one from the Walker. Seemed like some more firepower would be a likely idea for a man on his own.

This *pistolero* had done a trick I'd heard of before somewhere, dipping his spare cylinders in beeswax before pouching them. More I looked at that rig, more I thought about how big a chew I might have bit off here. When I spent the cylinder full of loads that was in the gun for practice, and realized how smoothed-down the piece was, how dead-flat accurate, I did still more thinking.

I tried hard to think which one of those yahoos I got this rig off of; kept coming up with Rogers himself.

The belt took some cutting down for me, but with the New Army high up on my right hip, the Walker in its usual cross-draw, and my good belt knife just below my right kidney where it always lived, I was better armed than the average war party.

My Henry held thirteen, the Walker six, The Remington six, and if I had to reload any of them I was in deep. All the same, I stuffed the old bandolier for the Henry full and slung it across my chest. With that long elk skin coat over all of it, I didn't look quite so much like the hardware peddler's wagon I was beginning to resemble.

All the rest of my loot was no account, though serviceable enough. One of the pistols was a Navy Colt, a model some folks still swear by, but it was dead in my hand, and I put it with the rest for dickering and selling.

Riding out, I recommenced to thinking about this sorry part of the world, or what I had learned of it, from trail and campfire talk.

Why, up in *Santa Fe,* the Mexican folk hold a *fiesta*, a holiday, every year, to celebrate the Pueblos and Apaches letting them come back after driving them out for puredee cruelty fifty years before. That is, their cruelty toward the Indians. And the Mex folk hated the Texans, and the Texans treated Mexes like second-class citizens in a place where they'd lived nigh two hundred years.

The hating was too deep for me in that country. Even the veterans who come back to Ohio from the War, like Pa hadn't, didn't look to be storing up hatred for lifetimes.

This was summer. Not only was it hot and dry, with the wind blowing dust all day and night; the *chamisa*, the rabbit bush, was blooming, and the junipers were putting out pollen.

Red and me both sneezed for ten minutes if we brushed up against that smelly, stinky stuff. You ain't *lived* until you have been up on a tall, sneezing horse on a rocky hillside, when you are about to blow your ownself out of the saddle!!

I was thinking how much I disliked the place when I rode into Las Cruces and up to Dutton's General Store.

Then Gwendolyn came out on the porch and that dusty place looked like competing with Heaven on a fair track.

She was wearing a sparkling clean white blouse with frills and lace up the front, and a pretty blue-and-white calico skirt. That outfit was just as big a miss at disguising her figure as the last one I'd seen her wearing. But she wasn't smiling this time.

"Mr. Kerrigan... I..."

"Call me Anse."

"Thank you...Anse...we've been hoping you'd come back. Uncle Paul is badly hurt, and we need you."

Somehow I knew, before she explained, what the problem was, and it made me feel some guilty. Rogers, of course. He'd come back in just a week, and caught old Mr. Dutton away from anybody or any weapons, and beat him bad, because he'd heard how good the old folks had treated me.

She was real quiet, showing me out back where there was a big loading dock and a little road for wagons. Back there, about two hundred yards across a field, was a house as nice as any I had seen in that country. It was of boards, built like houses back home.

Just as she was showing me into the bedroom where her Aunt and Uncle were, she said, low, "Anse, please call me Gwen?" Then she slipped away, still moving like a ship under sail, all smooth and sweet.

"Mr. Kerrigan! We'd been hoping..."Mrs. Dutton had tears in her eyes, and old Paul Dutton looked like a piece of meat someone had thrown to the dogs. Looked like he might lose his right eye, and the ear on the other side had been taken half off, from the look of the bandage. He was propped up in bed and he had a cast on his right arm.

"Yes, Ma'am?" Just then the door out in the kitchen slammed, and I heard boots coming across the boards. I had the Walker out and eared back, and this time I was carrying six live cylinders. Desperate to get the shooting out of the room with the old folks, I jumped into the kitchen...where I found myself looking over my barrel at Gwen and three bad-startled older men I'd never seen before. No, one of them was the barkeep from the saloon, without his white apron.

"Well, he's certainly alert and aggressive enough!" That turned out to be the doctor, and the other man was Minister of the Baptist Church. A couple more minutes, and we were joined by a priest, the man who ran the livery, and an undertaker. The barber was said to be coming, and the lady who run the post office and did sewing on the side.

They wanted them a Sheriff.

CHAPTER VIII

T he minister was up front about it, at any rate. "Ordinarily, you understand, a town looks for someone older, simply because younger men seem to be more apt to fight than to talk things out...but this situation calls for a proven fighter, and you've already shown you'll avoid killing when you can."

"Of course, judging from past performance, you constitute some competition for Father Rafael and myself," The minister and the priest grinned at each other. "But we really don't mind competition in the Lord's work." It took me a minute there to recall my game with the praying and singing, and I blushed some, and Gwen giggled. It was a nice giggle.

Old Dutton sounded awful raspy, but he was clear. "We'll pay you forty a month; give you a room in this house to stay in, and all your meals."

Same house as Gwen? They had themselves a boy, without any money at all...

"Will you pay for my ammo? It took me three months to get enough together to restock just recent..." The Undertaker and the doctor snorted, and Gwen, for some reason, had to bite her handkerchief just then.

"All the ammunition you use, no questions asked." Mrs. Dutton was firm, and none of the menfolks made to gainsay her. "Will you take the job?"

"Just one other thing..."

They all looked kind of exasperated, and I understood, because those were generous terms for an experienced, full-grown man then and there, and I was feeling stupid about that last little twitch of greed. But I needed to make this clear. "If I'm Sheriff, I am the *Sheriff*. I run myself. I don't get put out where someone else thinks I ought to be. My Pa got himself killed that way, probably."

It taken them a minute. But there it was, clear and plain, and the barkeep put it to them that if I was good enough to hire, I was good enough to be my own general.

I had to ask one last question. "When I get shut of Rogers and his bunch, do I still have a job?"

"We have seen what happens to a town without law enforcement. Of course." Old Man Dutton was the head rooster here, seemed like. Everybody nodded. Then they all shook my hand and sifted out of there.

Old Mr. Dutton looked like he was about to fold. Mrs. Dutton was fussing over his pillows and giving him what looked like a big glass of whiskey. I stepped into the kitchen just as Gwen was saying goodbye to all those people, and she turned around and blushed something fierce, because of me being maybe a bit close.

"Gwen, where is that livery place?" She looked at me, straight across, and I could see her brace so's not to step back. She fluffed some, like a hen bein' brave.

"Why, it's... it's almost three quarters of a mile... we have a little shed and a corral..."

"Still have to get some feed, if I keep them here. And is there a jail? Any set of laws for the town?"

She seemed a bit flustered at all the questions, and maybe they weren't the questions I should have been asking, but I had me a job needed some attention paid to it.

The jail was the other side of a little gulch, over behind the biggest saloon, where that big bartender had come from. I left Mule and Bridget the donkey in the corral, and all my gear in the Duttons' feed and shelter shed, and rode over there.

The place was one big cell, about ten by eight, with a metal front of riveted bars, and a front office was really the other half of the room, with a desk had one leg on a hunk of rock and a chair that had seen better days. A little tiny pot-bellied stove with a dirty coffee pot on it had a poker and ash shovel alongside. A tin cup hung on a rusty nail. The front door was open, flapping and slamming in the wind. The cell was locked, but the key was in the lock. There was a stained bucket in the cell. It was a little *adobe* building, made out of mud and straw like all those little buildings in that part of the world. The privy out back was mostly full, and rickety topside. In that country, nothing made of wood ever seems to rot, it just gets harder and harder. A little pile of firewood sat alongside the jail; looked to be juniper and cedar.

They had never been lime used in that outhouse, and the atmosphere was kinda thick around it. Fact of the matter, the jail itself didn't smell too good.

Inside the one drawer of the desk I found a badge and another key; that fit the front door. I put the badge on my shirt like I'd seen sheriffs and constables do here and there. In an apple crate under the desk were some padlocks with keys and a long piece of chain and some ratchet-bar handcuffs and a lead-weighted sap, what some folks call a blackjack. I put the door key and sap in my coat pocket, and left the place locked.

Gwen had the General Store open again. She was watching me from behind that counter, looking so pretty I near walked into a post was helping to hold up the roof. I put together a broom, a little can of stove black, some matches, a great big wood bucket, a dipper, a tablet of paper, and a pencil. Then I came to a section of mining supplies.

Way back in my travels, in Kentucky, I worked blasting and pulling stumps for a couple of months, until my employer's fondness for his own fine whiskey made the use of explosives riskier than it needed to be and I taken to the trail again. But I had learned how to use the tools of blasting. I put ten sticks of dynamite, a coil of fuse, some caps, a pair of cap pliers and a handled bit on the counter.

"I would appreciate if you'd add this pile up separate."

I never saw a girl so much taken with biting her handkerchief.

"I suppose this is...ammunition?"

"Yes, Ma'am."

"And the rest?"

"Amenities of the jail of a civilized community."

She was like to bite through that thing, seemed like to me.

"And are you providing those amenities out of your own pocket?" She sure was pert.

"Seems to me I only got permission to spend town money on ammo. But I am putting no man in a cell without water to drink, nor without a fire, cold nights."

She wasn't all bubbly, of a sudden. "Of course not!"

Still, she looked questioning at the pencil and tablet.

"For accounting and records and such."

"Mr... Anse, you can read and write?" She sounded kind of startled.

"I can read and write and figure sums. I read the Bible through a couple times, and *Gulliver's Travels*, and *Godey's Lady's Book*," she was chewing on that handkerchief again, "and newspapers when I could get them. Haven't had call to write nor figure for a while now." She was looking at me like she hadn't really seen me before.

"Aunt Immy will be serving dinner in about another hour. Will you be there?"

Dinner. In a house. With ladies. All of a sudden I was worried serious.

"If I have to be busy, don't wait for me, ma'am. I got to get a handle on this sheriff business quick-like." I paid her for the jail supplies, and went out of there.

I led Bridget with her casks to the jail, after I filled them at the Duttons' well, and then led Bridget with a load of hay from the livery to Duttons' shed, and just as I was feeding those three hay-burning nuisances, Mrs. Dutton stuck her head out the back door of the house and called "Supper!"

The Duttons' kitchen was fancier than any I had ever been in. They had them a water pump in the side porch, with a couple of basins set into a counter for washing, and a wood cook stove had a water reservoir in it, and warming ovens above, and they had cabinets, what they call pie-safes, with tin sheets on the front, all pierced artistic-like with nail holes too small for flies to get through. They had bins for flour and such beneath a big counter for rolling out dough. A rack of pots and pans hung up above the stove, and a cupboard had real china dishes in it.

I taken off my hat, and washed my hands and face without being reminded, but Gwen asked me soft-like, "Do you need *all three* guns at the table, Anse?" And so I shucked all but the Walker, and Gwen looked like she needed to bite her handkerchief some more, but she didn't.

"Mr. Kerrigan, would you say the Grace, please." Mrs. Dutton was matter of fact about it, but I was some took back.

"Your house, Ma'am."

"Mr. Dutton is too ill to sit at table, and it is something best done by a man."

I couldn't argue with the lady at her own table, and there were smells seemed like I had never smelled before, so I prayed earnest.

"Lord, give us this day our daily bread, and make all of our Enemies into Friends. Amen."

Gwen and Mrs. Dutton was looking at me some astonished. "That prayer was my Ma's. She called it a training prayer."

Mrs. Dutton just smiled nice and passed a basket of biscuits that was trying to float away, they were so light, and a dish of butter, and then passed a tureen of gravy, a big bowl of beans with bacon in them, a fancy bowl of jam with a cover had a hole for the little spoon, a big platter of steaks had been coated with flour before frying, and a bowl of canned stewed tomatoes. I come near to bawling, it had been so long since I had seen so much food of so many kinds all in one place.

I tried to mind my manners, but once I bit into one of them biscuits, they was no holding back, because I hadn't had no food all day, and I hadn't had no meal like this since Ma was well and Pa was still to home. By and by I looked up and seen Gwen looking hard put to keep in her laughing. I had me a biscuit in a death grip with one hand and a fork of steak in the other, and was having some trouble with the fork, because I hadn't used one for a couple of years. Mrs. Dutton smiled again, and said "A man gives the best compliment to the cook with his appetite for the cooking."

"Mighty good, Ma'am." It was some muffled, but sincere.

I felt like lines of strength and angel-song were going down all my limbs. When I couldn't hold any more, and was beginning to think I might have overestimated my capacity, Gwen smiled real sweet, and said, "Shall I serve the pie now or after dishes, Aunt Immy?"

I was plain terrified I might have to turn down... pie! But Mrs. Dutton thought we should do dishes first, which decision saved me an awful responsibility.

I dried dishes, taking more care than I did with loading the Walker. Gwen was next to me and it was hard to keep from just sniffing her hair or something else wouldn't have been acceptable manners.

And then they served pie made with dried apples, and coffee. I looked at that coffee some frightened, because of what happened the last time I tried it, but then I thought about all the Sheriff work I needed to get done, and drank it and was happy to have it.

"Gwen will show you to your room, Mr. Kerrigan. I have to look in on Paul; he was a bit feverish earlier. Good Night."

"Good Night, Ma'am, and thank you for the meal. I... ain't had none like it for a long time."

Gwen took me down a hall at the back of the house, and showed me into a room like I had never been in before. A bed centered the room, with a mattress of feathers, and sheets, and pillows, and three blankets. And there was a chamber pot under the bed with a cover, a copper basin set in a little table, that I later found out they called a commode, with a big pitcher sitting in the bowl, and an oval mirror up on a swivel. A corner had a big drape hung acrost it for a closet, and pegs set into the walls for hanging things on. The window had *glass* in it.

Gwen, she stood in the hall, and blushed some, looking kind of embarrassed. "The privy is out there, and that side is for the gentlemen."

"Now, that is some fancy. Two holes?"

Gwen went red. And formal, all to once. "No, *Mr. Kerrigan*, just two sides...and Aunty Immy serves breakfast at sunrise and twenty."

'Meaning?"

"Twenty minutes after sunrise." She braced up some, and gave me a fair blast, chin up and voice resonant..."*Try* not to use dynamite during the hours of sleep."

I could see as how she was avoiding giggling with an act of will. I decided to test it some.

"And if I just *have* to relieve my feelings with some gunfire, is that forbidden to me, too?" I tried to sound indignant.

She rose to the challenge, managed to do it straight-faced. "Just...restrain yourself for a few hours, Mr. Kerrigan."

I grinned like I'd done at those steaks earlier, after a fast, and said, "Oh, a few hours...."

She turned red, and fled the field.

I sauntered over to the saloon, letting Red eat and rest. When I came to the doors, I saw two of them fellows had been with Rogers was at the bar, talking loud and bullying at the barkeep, who was red and stressed-looking. So when I went in it was with my Henry at my shoulder, and walking direct to them. I put the barrel in the face was turned to me, and used my boot to inform the other one of my presence. I caught the barkeep's face for a minute and he was having a hard time looking neutral.

"You know how. Put them down, belts and all." Choice wasn't in it. I was serious as all get out, and they had no room to maneuver, none at all.

There was no way I was going to take two men, who had to be really irritated at me, out into the dark with them having any chance. "Now the boots." One of them started to complain, and I asked him direct, "Were you there when Mr. Dutton was beaten?" I taken aim between his eyes.

"No...No I wasn't."

"Good. Then take off your belt, put it through the loops on your boots. Do it slow." All around us, the folks was humming, and I asked the room, "Anybody object to this arrest?"

One skinny, bearded old coot, off in the corner, sneered and spit, missing the spittoon by a long ways. "You got no authority, you wet-a'hind-the-ears..."

I flipped the coat lapel aside, letting him see my badge, and slapped the Henry into my left, drawing the Walker with my other hand, and cocking it to cover my first two. "You shuck your gun belt and your boots too."

"Why?!" He was real indignant.

"Interfering with an officer of the law during a lawful arrest. Shuck them or I will leave you laying here for Mr. Lazlo." That was the name of the undertaker from the town council.

He shucked.

I asked the barkeep to hold gun belts and boots for me and I had a helpful cowboy tie those three men together at their necks with their own belts, real clumsy, but enough to slow them down if one of them lunged for me.

It was a long way acrost that little gulch in the dark, and those fellas swore fierce on account of the little tiny cactuses all over the ground. All of them were limping by the time we got to the jail. I locked them up in the cell, and they were yelling mean when I slammed the gate, leaving them to bare walls and a floor with just a little straw on it. But I spent the time to point out the amenities: a water bucket, with its dipper, outside the bars, and the other one inside, and to give them hope. "You got five days and five nights to become better men." I just spoke that, without thinkin', as it seemed right for a sentence for harrassin' a barkeep. "After that, you two," pointing to the two with whom I had had previous words, "can leave town alive and permanent, and you, there, with the tobacco dribbling down, you can show more respect for the law." I had another thought about then. That adobe is soft stuff, really. "Now, all of you put your trousers and your shirts out through the bars." No need to leave them with pocket knives and such.

They weren't going do it, but I pointed out that I had a stove, wood, water, and a pot...and they all needed bathing. All of those stinky, salt-crusty things came out. After I checked out the pockets, and noted down everything, and put it all in the desk drawer, I gave back trousers to the one had no long underwear. It was only decent.

On the way back across that gulch, I thought hard about taking prisoners around in the dark, and how I needed a lantern and some other things. This was a full moon. I had been lucky, and I had not planned careful enough for a professional lawman.

I put that clothing to air on a salt cedar was trying to live in that gulch. We called them tamarisks to home, but they took to this country real good.

The barkeep gave me all I had left with him, and he was a fine figure of a man, with upstanding mustaches, hair slicked back and gleaming, sleeves of his boiled shirt held up with blousing bands...all in all a fine figure of a bartender, and I asked him to talk in a back room so I would have some information about my prisoners, and knowledge of another door to the saloon, and so on. He shook my hand sincere, and thanked me, and I went back to my fine room. That supper had settled in nice and I was comfortable and happy.

When I sidled into the kitchen, with boots and belted guns hanging off both arms, Mr. Dutton was there, sitting up at the table, and looking better.

"Evening, sir."

He grinned some, which looked plumb awful, because of his split lips and torn-up face. "Have you had a good evening?"

"Jonathan Trevor and Delancy Vernon and Albert McGrath are guests in the jail, and I *got* to get a lantern."

"There is a spare on the back porch, where I hope you will keep those boots, and I am very happy you have proved to be as... energetic about this as I told the council you would be."

"Glad to hear that, sir. Was Rogers alone when he done this to you?"

"That bayou trash, Vernon, was there, and he had a good laugh every time Rogers put in a boot."

"You folks have a Justice of the Peace, or a Judge comes around, or a set of town laws?"

He looked at me with the eye was working, cocked over to one side like a thoughtful chicken. "Your position is appointive, by a town council which is largely informal, and there is no judge closer than Prescott at this time. Gwen tells me you can write. Draw up a set of town ordinances you think you can make stick, and I will offer suggestions, if that doesn't offend you, *Sheriff,* and we will have a meeting and pass on them. If we have to have a trial, then we will put together twelve decent folk and make it an honest one." He was teasing me some there, but it was friendly teasing.

I realized I was a bit further out on a limb than I would have cared for, but at least I had the town people with me.

"Any idea where Rogers keeps himself when he's not in town?"

"There is a ranch well north, where he is apparently welcome. He hasn't shown himself here since he did this to me, because even if no one here has a background like his, with Quantrill, a number of people can shoot rifles well, and will, if they see him again." I felt my stomach drop out, because I remembered now where I'd heard of that cylinder-dipping trick.

"Yes, Sir. I better be saying good night."

I was careful to put the boots out on the porch.

There was a little towel with that basin, so I cleaned off some before bed, and then noticed a nightgown was laying acrost the pillows. I had never worn any such thing in my life, but figured it was meant to spare the sheets.

The room was lighted with a candle, which I blew out before I positioned my Henry under the window, the New Army under the pillow, the Walker in the corner by the door, and moved the bed careful about six feet over toward the outside wall.

In the morning I had plenty of warning with the chickens and all. When I was a youngster, the sound of roosters serenading the sunrise was so common it never woke me up. Now, after months in the high-up mountains, the bray of the he-chickens brought me sitting upright.

I was up, dressed, using moccasins because it was way before sunrise, and out to the gentlemen's side of the privy early, fed my four-footed family and shifted my bed back where it had been, and then I taken that pitcher into the kitchen, after hot water for shaving.

Gwen was wearing a nightgown her own self, with one of them bed jackets. She kind of scrunched up and leaned into the wall. I apologized. Seemed like whatever was happening with ladies, it was always safest to apologize right off, even before thinking out what might be the matter.

"Why, Sorry, Miss Gwen, I just want some hot water here..." I have never figured this one out. That gown and jacket were about three times more successful at covering all of the interesting terrain than the clothes she wore to work at the store... why was she taking on so? Her hair was all tousled up, and beautiful...but she was making real flustered motions like she was trying to comb her hair and sew buttons onto that nightgown at the same time. It was delightful to watch.

I got me a couple-three cups of near boiling water from the reservoir on the stove, and retreated quiet. I used my razor, and then I neatened up some and was ready when "Breakfast!" sounded down the hall.

Gwen was pink, all through breakfast, which was eggs and pancakes and bacon and coffee. I hadn't had bacon for two years save for what I had taken from that coyote-hatted man, and no pancakes for three. It was hard to keep from hugging old Mrs. Dutton. The Mr. was abed, and we had very little talk. Mrs. Dutton looked pale and peaked, and Gwen turned plumb red every time we locked eyes. I noticed she had combed her hair all smooth, and done some other things I never figured out, because she looked about twenty now, and earlier she had looked about twelve. Well, her face had.

I saddled Red, and made my way to the jail, not even thinking of helping with the dishes till I was there.
"Up and out."

They were no way happy about the chain locked around their necks so they had to stand right close to each other, nor about the shovel and pick I made them use to start digging a new outhouse out back of the jail. Fact was, when I put them in the shade at noon and brought a water cask to refill their drinking bucket, one made bold to complain.

Vernon's choice of language was crude, and I am not going to repeat it, but I pointed out that he could walk away if he could chew through the chain, and dodge my bullets successful. He shut up for a while.

The spitter, name of McGrath, said, "I never seed yore badge, there, Sheriff. I wouldn'ta spoke that way had I knowed you was a lawman."

Now, I took him prisoner as a tactic to make it look really expensive to challenge me. I had been feeling guilty ever since.

"Is that the truth, Mr. McGrath?"

"Yes, sir, it is."

"Well, then, let me unlock that chain." I took him inside, had him sign for his pocket stuff, directed him polite to the salt cedar, and told him he could get his boots and gun at the saloon, tomorrow morning. He hobbled off, looking properly humble.

Those other two was surly, but the Henry had a big eye looking at them, and I got a fair afternoon's work out of them. After I put them back in the cell, I threw them a good big piece of jerky each, and refilled the water bucket. I have always believed in fair pay.

"Sheriff?" It was Vernon again.

I looked at him careful, and listened. "You know, Captain Rogers is a' gonna' kill you like a dog, don'cha?" He was grinning and taunting me, sneering and hoping to scare me.

I looked back at him. "Why, no, Mr. Vernon, I think that's kind of unlikely."

I went to my home for the night, thinking, *Captain Rogers*?

CHAPTER IX

"**A**nse...Uncle Paul told me you had prisoners at the jail. How are you feeding them?" I thought it was sweet of her to be so concerned.

"I have about four hundred pounds of jerky I was going to sell. That's plenty for short-staying guests."

"I...see. And what are you doing at that jail? At the store I was hearing metal on rock all day."

"Jail needs a new privy dug. After that it will need a well way off the other side, the streets need leveling and tamping, hitching posts are in short supply…"

She looked downright shocked. "You're having those men do that kind of work on just *dried meat*?! That seems cruel."

"I have been working just as hard, often on less food, for more than a year."

Old Mrs. Dutton looked up from her plate and nodded, like she was hearing something she knew already.

"It's not cruel, it's just not pleasant. I feel as how jail shouldn't be a pleasant experience."

"But when you are so hard... it means all of us are doing it, because you represent us."

"Gwen, when those men sat outside the store and bothered everyone, and when they scared off your last Sheriff, and when they beat your poor uncle, wasn't that... hard, too? When they put me in a place where I had to take shame or fight, wasn't that kind of cruel? They had none of them ever seen me before, neither."

She looked real sad, and finally said, "I agree. But if you have prisoners on Sunday, will you let them rest? And maybe...let them have some better food?"

I was eating fried chicken with biscuits and honey and butter, and I was inclined to be nice to the world. Also, I was remembering the table manners Ma had taught me away back, and I wasn't so embarrassed nor nervous anymore. So I agreed. "No work and some better food." And then I had a thought, and I added, "And maybe the sky-pilots can come and hold Sunday School too!"

Gwen looked at me some suspicious, but I kept my mouth wrapped around a piece of chicken so she couldn't see me grinning.

I worked at going round the town on Red two or three times a day, just looking and getting down to talk with folks sometimes. Any time I left those prisoners I chained them in shade with the water bucket, and they had nice long breaks because I like meeting folks. I started to pick up some Spanish and ladies and kids would wave.

Turned out there were two hungry horses, wandering with loose reins...they belonged to those reprobates in the jail, of course. I got horses and saddles, a couple saddle guns, and, in one saddlebag, another of those fine '58 New Army Remingtons...the union one, this time, and a spare cylinder. Bet I knew where those had been headed. Red and Mule showed those other animals who was boss right away.

The time came to turn those polecat friends of Rogers loose, and by then I had three garden-variety fighting drunks, one of whom had emptied his pistol indiscriminate whilst in his cups, and a little skinny Mexican kid had been seen sneaking into a storage shed. He was arrested for me, by a whole bunch of angry folks, all shouting in Spanish. He didn't have any boots to take away, and he was obvious real glad to get the jerky I fed him. I made sure he got all of it he could eat. His clothes were rags, and he looked to be a bit younger than me. His name was *Emilio*. He worked so hard and willing that after two days I didn't chain him when I was with the work crew, just pointed him at a job. He knew about adobe, and the jail got re-plastered inside and out. I took to bringing him biscuits and honey from my own breakfast and lunch. He was some kind of proud, but any good treatment just melted him. I figured alla his problem was bein' cold and hungry…and down the road I proved to be right.

We had us a couple of talks, Emilio and me, and turned out he'd lost his family to a raiding party of Yaquis, those real fierce cousins of the Apache, around a place called Nacozari, in Sonora, down Mexico way, a couple of years back. He hadn't got away with anything at all, and had been living hand to mouth and almighty rough most of the time since. Being pot boy for a cook working with some stock was being drifted North to *Neuvo Mexico* had got him into the area of Las Cruces, and taught him some English, but left him altogether nothing to live on when the herd went onto pasture and the outfit broke up.

He wasn't looking for sympathy, but you could tell he didn't want to be taken for a thief. He'd just been trying to find a place to sleep out of the wind, and maybe something to chew on better than *tunas*, those prickly pear fruit, that had been all he'd had to eat for days before.

Vernon was still mean and nasty despite my sincere efforts to allow him to improve. When he realized he had lost his gun, gun belt, and his boots for the second time, *and* a horse and saddle gun, he said words to me he should have been holding a gun for. So when I let his sidekick, Trevor, limp off to get his shirt and hat out of the salt cedar, I kept Vernon in the cell. I put the work crew to digging and Emilio to adobe plastering outside, and stepped back in to administer Justice.

Vernon was looking at me some scared. "Vernon, you are a want-to-be bad man. I would haul you out and whip you within an inch of your life, but I don't want to waste the time, or chance getting hurt, because I got too much to do. So I am going to give you some time to think about how you laughed when Old Man Dutton was getting beat up by your friend Rogers."

The water bucket was out with the crew, because it was already in the high nineties at seven in the morning. I filled that potbellied stove with straw and juniper, lit it, took a water cask with me, and set about guarding my chain gang.

I purely hated that part of the job. It meant I couldn't do anything else, and even if I brought some little hand work or sewing to do, I didn't dare pay too close attention to it.

After an hour, I chained them all in the shade for a break, and went in to refill the stove. Vernon was lying in the furthest corner of the windowless cell, panting and sweating. I filled that stove up full again, almost falling over from breathing the hot air, and went out quick. That outside door fitted pretty good, for being old wood in that climate.

By the end of the morning, Vernon didn't have anything left to sweat with, and he fell down flat a couple of times on his way out the door. "You tell Rogers and the rest of your low-life friends that Las Cruces is just a foretaste of hell for your kind." I know he heard me, but he didn't say anything. Maybe he couldn't. His skin was all dry and his eyes had trouble blinking. There were some puddles in the gulch. He'd live. I don't think he liked me, though.

There was a town council meeting that next week. Mr. Dutton held it in his kitchen this time, as he was getting a bit better. Besides, so many folks showed up they couldn't have fit into the Duttons' bedroom again.

I read my report, names and time served, supplies bought, and weapons confiscated. Those horses got taken because I'd warned those fellas personal while I was a private citizen, so I didn't include them in the report. Mr. Dutton looked at me close when I finished, and quirked his torn up lips. Couldn't tell was he upset or not.

A few questions about the cost of keeping prisoners come up, because it seems they hadn't all realized that I couldn't just shoot all the bad fellas dead. Letting them know about the jerky I was contributing and asking the minister and the priest to come talk to a captive audience regular helped too. Telling about the new privy, and plastering, and the well that had been started made them sit up and take notice. And when I proposed using proceeds from impounded weapons to pay for jail necessities, it went over good. That was nice, because I would get my money back for the supplies I had bought already. One man, the freight foreman, talked about money fines or bail, but everyone agreed, without any sort of judge or justice, that was too hard to do. I pointed out that when I put someone in the jail, it was someone who shouldn't be able to stay loose right then just because he had money in his pocket.

Fact was, several people wanted me to confiscate the guns off everyone I jailed; but I held firm to only doing that with folks who shot them or threatened with them. "If it doesn't look fair, it won't be something I can keep up." Everyone was pretty happy how peaceful things were getting, so they went along.

The town rules were simple, and had to do with decent behavior let everyone get some sleep and feel safe. I wrote them, and like he said, Mr. Dutton made some suggestions. I added all of his suggestions. Mr. Dutton was a man who thought straight. And he wrote a lot clearer than I did, back then.

That Baptist minister stood and preached to them prisoners for nigh on two hours starting at dawn every Sunday an' a couple noonings mid-week too. Why, sometimes he had them fellas on the edge of tears; especially when they had been up since near sunrise digging through rock. I think he was more effective than the jerky and lack of tobacco. The priest, Father Rafael, came over too, but he was a lot quieter and nicer to listen to, with all that Latin language just flowing on. I seldom had me any Catholics, but all the prisoners seemed to think of the priest as a comfort, which was a shame, far as I was concerned.

Saturday nights, I took my pot to the jail and put elk jerky to boil with onion and potatoes. That was Sunday breakfast, and I let them have a bowl each after the minister got done. I had promised Gwen.

I thought hard on it, an' the last day Emilio was a prisoner, I had him make a simple rope bed for the front office, and I bought a big mattress sack and stuffed it with hay. I bought a new, thick wool blanket, too. All them prisoners looked longing-like at that bed when I locked them into that bare adobe cell for the night.

His release day, I gave him one of those confiscated pistols with a gun belt, and gave him his pick of boots and knives, him looking like he couldn't believe he had got them.

After we went down to the creek and I'd let him use some soap I'd filched from Mrs. Dutton's laundry bucket, I took him to the store and introduced him to Gwen and to

Mrs. Dutton, and bought him a shirt like mine and a straw *sombrero*. He was panting and gasping with happy.

I made him a deal. He could stay in the jail office, and I'd let him use my pot and pan and make some potatoes and beans and stuff available to him, and the next prisoner job after the well could be another room for him to bunk in. I thought he was going to bust out crying, so I found something for the ladies to look at outside for a while until he came out and accepted the deal. He was upright and struttin', and I took care not to take any of the proud out of him. He would need every ounce of it.

So now I had me a swamper and guard, and somebody to make putting prisoners in and out a lot safer; also someone to teach me more useful Spanish. It didn't hurt that Emilio was a youngster it felt good to be good to.

Emilio did know how to make a pistol shoot, but that was all. He missed 'most all the time. He'd squinch up his eyes, and let fly whilst grinchin' and flinchin'. By and by, when I chanced to confiscate a ten gauge double-barrel shotgun used cartridges, I had the blacksmith cut it down short and gave it to Emilio for guarding with. It was impressive, because it was almost bigger than he was, and it was a lot more likely than a handgun to give him a chance if he was rushed.

Summer was over, and I wasn't having to arrest folks near as often. I assigned Emilio one of those confiscated horses and what was a better saddle than I had, and had some of the town council come and have a little ceremony, making him a deputy, official. The blacksmith cast him a badge from a silver dollar. I sold the other horse, and its gear, and had money for food for Emilio. We got the extra room done just before the first snow fell, late September. That was soon gone, but the wind was always cold, with whipping, icy dust sometimes as big as gravel. Emilio got himself his own outside door, so he didn't have to be smelling the cell all the time, but he still did cooking on the potbellied stove outside the cell, which went a long way toward reminding prisoners what they was missing. He had a door into the jail office, and I spent some money to put a solid pair of braces on that, so's he could bar that door solid. Also, I spent some money putting a little glass window in that door so he could glance at the prisoners without having to go in there. Once the cold weather came, we burned straw all over the inside floors to kill all the fleas and lice and their eggs our clientele had brought in. Then we replastered inside, so the jail smelled clean finally.

I borrowed Old Man Dutton's wagon, and with Mule in the traces and looking happy to have something to do, if a mule can be said to look happy, we went north out of town, ten miles or so, for wood. I buck-sawed ten full wagons of dead fir and *piñon,* and taken near to October to get it all to town, being deliberate real erratic about timing my trips. A couple times when we hadn't any prisoners, Emilio came along, and that made the work a lot faster. I put most of the wood at Dutton's house, and piled the rest alongside the jail. Got a couple deer, too, for house venison and so Emilio could have fresh meat for a while. After the last trip I was standing in the corral, having brushed Mule down good, and he came and put his head over my shoulder, like he used to do when I was little, and I stroked his muzzle, gone mostly gray. I guess he felt good doing something after so long idle.

I sold some confiscated guns and knives and things and gave Emilio forty dollars for clothing and more blankets.

And we put deep straw in the cell, kept the stove going all the time. We still worked prisoners hard, but brought them in every couple of hours so we wouldn't kill them off. We let them wrap their feet and heads in rags and straw while they were outside, too.

Every night I moved my bed from its daytime position, and I tried going a little different route everywhere, all the time. I never stood in windows, and always guarded prisoners from a sheltered spot if I could. In all that time, Rogers never showed.

We heard of him. He killed a man up in Santa Fe, and he and his crowd stole from a family of movers up around Bernalillo; beat the husband bad.

One day, finally, it was so cold I put on my Storm Stopper.

Gwen was just finishing batter for a cake, looking pretty and flushed, wearing that grey dress that called all sorts of features to my attention. She still near floored me just sighting her, after months living in the same house.

She broke out laughing as I walked into the kitchen with my empty bears brushing both sides of the doorway.

"What *is* that? A haystack of hair!?!"

I twirled around like a little girl showing off a new dress. "It's my Storm Stopper; two big bear hides and a *lot* of work."

"Why, it's big enough for *two* people." She was running her fingers through the long fur, and I just flared the thing out and whipped it around us. It was heavy enough, it pressed her in against me, firm. "Sure is."

She wriggled her head up and outa the lapels, laughing but looking startled. We were playing... and then we weren't. I kissed her. I could no more help myself than I could stop the snow.

She froze for a second, and then she was cooperatin' enthusiastic-like.

"Anse, for a man who moves so fast, you are really *slow*!" She was firmer against me than my storm stopper had any blame for.

I got to the jail kind of late that morning. That Gwen girl just played hell with my plans!

CHAPTER X

That was a pretty nice winter , by and large. I had to make one change in my kit, though. Gwen said I had to put a lining in my Storm Stopper because we seemed to walk most places together in it, and the leather side of the bear hides was too raspy. She even picked out the fabric, something called velveteen they had bolts of in the store because the Indian folk liked it. We sat close all the time we put it in together. We worked in the kitchen or on the porch, and Mrs. Dutton kind of snorted and giggled all to oncet every time she saw us sewin' together. Gwen thought it was real comfortable to go to the store wrapped up in bearskins and with a friendly warmer. In fact, she sort of required me to provide ferry service morning and night. I didn't resist none. I explained my variations of routes to her, and as a result, sometimes going to or coming back from the store took us a long time. In fact, we varied routes over an entire town and its nearby trails, when the snow was thin enough. We got to knowing each other good, and I was liking her more every day. It was like an empty place in me was filling up.

Funny about that fabric. It was a silly thing done to please a girl. And it come to save my life.

I did drop in on Emilio every day and my Spanish was getting good enough for real talking. Come to find out, my deputy was just fifteen and hadn't been but fourteen when I first met him. And then I learned the difference 'tween birthdays and name days so he was really sixteen by my way of thinking. But for a while there I was feeling guilty about risking a young 'un. He got to be better looking as he put on some meat. Not that Emilio'd been ugly, but with some flesh on him, he wasn't looking so desperate hungry. He treasured his little wisp of a mustache, and the Latin girls started looking at him.

Gwen was on me about my casual speaking in English, and sometimes, if she hadn't been so pretty her lessoning would have been hard to take. But my English was getting to be proper even faster than my Spanish.

'Twas Sunday night, and I was just coming across the gully, bringing a loaf of bread and a covered bucket of soup Mrs. Dutton had sent for Emilio. With no moon and most of the snow blown away, it was black as the inside of a cow. There was ice on the little cactuses and the skeletons of rabbit bush, so when I came across the creek I moved slow, in order not to slip.

Emilio hadn't any prisoners just now and I was bettin' he could use some company.

Horses went by in a rush, hard ridden by quiet men. I nearly spilled the soup, gettin' back below the bank. But vittles stopped mattering real fast, on account of how gunfire tends to suppress my appetite.

There were at least ten of them, and all of them were shooting, some with two weapons goin' at once. The gleam of light around the jailhouse door became a starburst as the door splintered under dozens of hits. In the little pause as empty pistols got traded for full ones, I saw gunfire flare from inside, and the riders milled around some, but none of them went down. The muzzle flashes among the dark milling shapes of men and horses lit them up almost constant, and made my eyes water.

So Emilio was alive, probably because his room hadn't a window on the front side of the jail. If there'd been any prisoners though, they'd be chopped to pieces by now.

"Yu! Yu fancy-dressin' som'beetch! Yu come out and traih me lahk a mayunn!"

It was Rogers. And he was some worked up.

One curve down from the gully crossing was where I kept some things I didn't want at the house or jail. I moved down there, taking short little steps to avoid snagging my toes, or making noise, got down on my knees and pulled rocks off the crate I'd set into the bank.

Dynamite likes it cool.

The frozen ground felt like icy iron under my knees and added to the cold feeling from the fear.

I filled the front of my shirt with pre-capped and fused sticks. That was prickly, because I'd wrapped some barbed wire thick around a half dozen of them, filing notches every few inches of wire as I wrapped. I made sure the matches in the fruit jar was in the crate were dry.

I was cold mad, now. These men had tried to kill me and Emilio without warning. I owed them no mercy, but I felt bad about the horses.

The Storm Stopper showed none of the pale leather inside, on account of that velveteen, and the soft stuff made it silent against my other clothing and gear. It let me ghost up to about fifty feet and then I turned around and hunkered down so the big robe made a tent, put my face in the front. When I struck a match, I cringed, but no light got out, or they'd surely have shot me then.

I lit two wire-wrapped sticks, and two more bare ones, made sure the fuses were going, dropped the match into my private patch of snow... if the fuses burned true, I had one minute.

I straightened and turned to see that two were off their horses, moving up alongside the jail door, and the others were lined up and making to climb down. I started throwing.

The two plain sticks, lighter, went out on the ends of the lines and the wire-wrapped ones went toward the middle of the bunch. "Keyriist! Lookout!" came from one of 'em seeing the fuses arcin' in, and I drew the two '58 Remingtons I was carrying these days. I gave them a rolling volley, turning my head back and forth with each cock and hammer drop, trying to get a knockdown on either end of their line. I emptied my cylinders. One stick went off toward their center and I whirled and lay down flat, while the others blew. I felt some tugging on the robe, but nothing bit me, so I moved off fast, positively delighting in the screaming and carrying on behind me.

I dropped cylinders and replaced them on the run, curved around to come back in ...and stopped right where I was.

Emilio was inside, and I couldn't get to him right now, whether or not he was hit. I wasn't where I had been when I had been making muzzle flashes, and they couldn't have tracked me by sound. I could barely hear shots going off, and realized *I* was near deaf from a blast fifty, sixty feet away from me. *They'd* had those hunks of giant powder in their hip pockets!

So I held still, crouched low and trying with all my might to resemble something harmless.

By and by, I picked out movement and began to sort out the noise. Screaming and cursing and groaning was going on like you never heard. I took little notice of the ones yelling. I was more concerned with the ones had been on foot and with their weapons in hand.

I tried not to hear the horses was screaming. It didn't work.

There was still light from the jail door, and against that I caught movement in a low spot was maybe twenty feet from me. I moved back a bit, shuffling and crouching, and went to a knee to bring my horizon up. Yep, there was a man's arm and shoulder. He was laying there, waiting for someone to move in on the hurt ones or the jail. Trouble was, I had gone out a good seventy-five yards in my first retreat, and he was revealed as he surely hoped I would be.

So I had one man close, and a bunch down, hurt or otherwise, in a clump another seventy yards away.

I didn't want to be predictable, using the same tactic all the time, but the situation called for the use of superior force, and there ain't much force superior to dynamite. I tented up again, and by feel trimmed a fuse to less than a inch, leaving another two the original length. Then I gripped them so as not to mix them up, lit them and heaved the short-fused one into the low spot where I was being awaited. I flattened out quick, and was barely in time.

I went through that little swale, one pistol out in case there was anybody alive to dispute passage. There wasn't. I heard a horse charge away from over by the jail as I came out of the low spot and set to throw. The other two sticks went off about as soon as they landed among all the yelling and moaning .

And then I lay down right where I was, and rested my ears a while.

After a few minutes, I heard kind of feeble cursing, and another horse moved off. I didn't even look up. Any of them could move I *wanted* to get away just now. Ten to two in the dark of night was not odds I wanted to play with. In another hour the moon would be up.

Light came onto the land before the moon cleared the edge of the world. I held still and looked and listened. By the time the moon was above the horizon, I had at least six men spotted, with five of them showing movement, or at least appearing to breathe. One was lying across a dead horse. Both man and horse were torn open and obvious dead.

So two had gone away... or wanted me to think they had, and I had one man unaccounted for. But my count had been a quick one. Ten, as they say, was just a working number. So I held still some more. I could do that easy, and I confess that, with the Storm Stopper being as heavy and warm as it was, I near fell asleep for a little bit there. I startled out of that doze-nod ice-prickly scared.

The moon had moved across almost a third of the sky. A couple of hurt men were trying to help each other.

There was no more light from inside the jail. Either the lantern had burned empty or Emilio had got to it. I had no way of knowing which, until those wounded bandits made a bit too much noise, and Emilio's ten gauge went off from low down the splintered door. One of the hurt ones shrieked and fell, holding his head. This brought a few shots from the other wounded, and fire from the ground over by the gully. So that was where my missing lamb was grazing!

To get to that lone shooter I would have to circle out a couple hundred yards, because the moon was near full. He was out of range for throwing and the wounded or downed ones were between us.

I decided to use diplomacy. Being diplomatic, I spoke low and I did not move. "You coyotes can go stand right in front of the jail, without any weapons, and live. Or you can have a *case* of dynamite for breakfast. Choose." I was fibbin' because I had only a couple-three sticks left.

They started, and one turned and looked along his rifle like he wanted a target, but another one slapped his barrel down and growled, all bubbly and gasping, "Damn fool! Drop it!"

It took them a couple minutes to disarm and start moving. When their intentions were clear, I called, "Emilio! Keep your scatter gun on these critters, and if they shift, let go both barrels!"

Emilio sounded really glad to hear from me. "Si', Jefe!"

I distinct heard both the hammers on that monster go back, and so did the prisoners, because a couple flinched.

There were lanterns and noise now from the main street, a gathering there. I heard a voice giving crisp instructions. The doctor had been an army surgeon once.

Another horse took off, from within the gully. I could see the crouched rider, but it was almost a hundred yards... not pistol range.

By the time our townsfolk had arrived, with an amazing assemblage of weapons and lanterns, we had five miserable men in the cell. One would obvious not make it to morning. That was Jonathan Trevor; he should never have come back. Two more seemed to be totally deaf, one had a smashed leg, another crushed ribs; they all looked like someone had thrown dynamite at them, in fact.

Emilio had a bullet burn along his right jaw and bad splinters all along the top of his right shoulder and the right side of his face. Despite the screaming and pleading from the cell, Emilio got the doctor's attention first. When he had been probed, stitched, and was full of laudanum, the prisoners got fixed. I noticed that doc didn't give any laudanum to any of them except Trevor who was surely doomed, with a good hunk of missing insides.

"Anson, you are the best tactician I have ever heard of. But you have an imagination ought to be outlawed!" Doc snapped his case closed and went home.

CHAPTER XI

What with burying of bodies and gathering of weapons, it was late morning before I could go see Gwen. Taken me most of an hour to find my own dropped cylinders, and those bandits had left hardware all over a couple acres of ground.

Emilio went off and made arrangement with the livery to have three horses dragged 'way out of town.

Gwen was standing by the dough board in the kitchen. Her back was straight and she looked tight and trembly. She didn't face me when I come in.

I put my hands on her shoulders and turned her around. Her eyes were red and I could see she had been crying some.

I give her the bad news first. "Rogers got away." Her eyes got shocked and sad. I could see she had been hoping it was over.

"How many were they?"

"Twelve. Two were waiting out of town with fresh horses. They had it all done up like a raid, like Quantrill used to do them."

"You caught those two?"

"No, but one of them was real drugged last night..."

Her face sagged. "The one who died this morning?"

"Yep. Jonathan Trevor." She looked tired and sad.

"So Rogers and the other two who got away *really* got away, and he still has four men. Of course," I grinned a bit, "one or more of them may be some sick for a while."

She grabbed me hard, and I could feel her shaking.

I took her hands off me, gentle. "I got to fetch something."

I unwrapped Ma's quilt, and carried it into the kitchen spread over my arms. I swirled it around her like I done that bearskin robe that other time. She knew what it was, having seen me clean it a time or two, and her eyes were real big all of a sudden.

"Gwen, I think we should get married."

She went all still and looked in my eyes. When I wore boots, she had to look up just a tad bit. "I can get us a house built the Mexican way, and even have us a good kitchen like this..."

"You think I *care*?"

My heart dropped. "Why, I thought you kind of favored me thataway..."

"You...you darling idiot! I don't *care* where we live... but if you don't marry me fast, I'm going to explode!"

"Oh."

"And, Anson, we don't have to move..."

"I can't ask your aunt and uncle to..."

"This house, and the store, is half mine. My father and Uncle Paul were partners, not brothers... "Aunt" and "Uncle" are just my baby names for them!"

She was grinning now.

"If you want, we can put on another big bedroom."

I was some dislocated. And maybe that's why my deep-down worry popped out.

"No little 'uns with those chins...?" I felt the relief make my face go loose, like faces do when folks have a weight taken off their minds.

She gaped at me and then exploded laughing. We were still giggling when Mrs. Dutton come in, and both of us nigh strangled for fear she'd ask us to share the joke.

"Aunt Immy, we are going to get married."

The old lady stopped and nodded. "Well, it's about time!" She grinned sudden, and looked really amused for a minute. "You youngsters in any particular hurry?"

Gwen and me both blushed beet red right off. Then we looked at each other blushing and started laughing.

Finally, I got out, "No ma'am. Not that kind of hurry. But we don't want to be a long time to the event." Gwen nodded real firm.

So I got Emilio to recruit a couple of Mexican families did it for a living to build an adobe wing and porch onto the main house. Truth was, that was a lot cheaper than paying for lumber had to be waggoned in and put together by Anglo carpenters. Adobe made a warmer, quieter building. I had no idea of staying in that place for ever, but Gwen and I could be comfortable while we did. I did have to wagon-drag in some big logs for *vigas*, but nothing Mule couldn't handle.

Those prisoners were in a sad way. I made jerky and potato soup for them, and gave them a drink the Mexican folks made using *Tamarindo* pods.

All of them were hurt. I gave them a week to start healing and then the town held a trial. We held it there in the "dining room" of the big saloon because with the exception of the churches, there was no place else in town for so many people to get together at one time. And while pastor Jenkins offered his church, no one wanted to have a court of law in a holy place. It just didn't seem right.

Charges were attempted murder, assaulting law officers, destruction of public property, and recklessly discharging firearms. I hadn't any experience placing charges, but the

Doctor was more knowledgeable. "If they have done more than one, charge them with more than one."

We hadn't recourse to a prison. We had only the jail.

Mr. Dutton put it to them. He was up front with them. "We can hang you or we can flog you or we can work you for a long time. I'm personally inclined to tie you up and bullwhip you bloody and *then* hang you." The room kind of growled, and all those prisoners had the good sense to look scared.

Even I swallowed hard at that. Those men were all bruised and bandaged and one of them kept shaking his head like something was loose in there.

"I have a suggestion, folks." They all listened respectful. I had shown them what a real fight could be against bullies, and they were liking me for it just then.

"The man who set this up and planned it got away. These men are bandits and toughs.... but I really don't want to see them hang. I called on them to surrender on terms of letting them live. I would not like to have my word ignored." I looked at those broken-up men and a couple of them had the grace to look ashamed of themselves. "I think they should live real hard and do a lot of work for the town. Maybe a year of work. We can't afford to keep them for anything like a real prison sentence...and I'll undertake to make a year feel like ten." I glared some at my prisoners, and while they had been lookin' a bit relieved whilst I was speakin', they started in on apprehensive again.

There was some laughing. My program of jerky and hard labor was becoming a matter of local pride, and the townsfolk agreeing with it kind of helped my feeling of steady work in prospect. Proposing to Gwen had made me more thoughtful of such things.

"Deputy! Take em outside, please." 'Milio really liked being called by his title. He positive swelled up with pride when I used it.

Emilio gestured forceful with his scattergun, and the clattery bunch shuffled out the door, plumb pitiful in their long johns and chains and bandages and bare feet.

"Hold 'em close. We may yet have to hang 'em." I shut the door behind them.

Mr. Dutton called for a show of hands. Everyone on the council had come, everyone, including the ladies, voted. Nobody disagreed, save the Pastor Jenkins, to my surprise. But then, thinking of the kind of hellfire sermons he liked to give, I *shouldn't* have been surprised. Pastor Jenkins positive delighted in describing what awaited the unsaved. It was his favorite topic and he went into a lot of detail. I usually left him to preach at the cellful of prisoners while I waited outside, or lately, sat in with Emilio and played cards or practiced Spanish.

He was a big, red-faced man, and since he insisted on wearing a closed collar and a tie, he got redder along about midday, even in winter.

"These are thieves and murderers! They should never be free to harm innocent people again! It is to God they should answer, and it is our duty to put them in front of God's Judgment Throne . . ." He was startin' to bellow, like he did preachin', and folks shifted back some, 'cause it wasn't that big of a room.

The Doc cut him off kind of short. Doc didn't go to church, though he had a well-used Bible, I knew. I suspect he kinda disapproved of Pastor Jenkin's brand of Christianity. I know I was beginnin' to, my own self.

"This is a jury, and the way juries usually work, we'd vote on each charge and, if we had a judge, suggest a penalty to him. But we are also the town council, and don't *have* a judge, so we are just voting, and you are outvoted. Sheriff Kerrigan" he always used my formal name to others, which note of respect felt good, "has suggested a penalty within our means, and suitable for crimes in which only some of the *perpetrators* died." I knew the doctor knew more law than anyone in town except maybe Mr. Dutton. He had a whole shelf of books and he let me read them in his waiting room whenever I wanted, but he made me wash my hands first. He treasured those books. Sometimes we talked about things I come across in them and in a way Doc was giving me an education I had not had time or opportunity to get before.

Everyone spoke up at once for a minute there, and Mr. Dutton waved the room quiet, and flinched, because his right shoulder still hurt him a lot.

"Another show of hands, now the Reverend has spoken . . ."

There was one other hand stayed down this time, the postmistress's. She was at the church 'most every day, to put in flowers, or somethin'.

Mr. Dutton nodded at me and at the Doc, sour faced but satisfied.

"We are agreed, then. One year at hard labor for all of them."

I taken the opportunity to get in an argument for a regular salary for Emilio on account of how brave he had been in the fight at the jail. "He's riskin' his life for everyone, just ridin' herd on those low lifes. I couldn't have any time to patrol the town or anything if I didn't have him, and he makes everyone safer."

"Sheriff, we pay you good money, and you're worth it, but there are only ten of us paying you, and it is not easy for all of us." That was the postmistress/dressmaker lady. She was maybe fifty-odd, and talking around town, I'd learned the house she lived in was all she'd had when her husband got bit by a rattler a few years back. She scraped by, but I looked around and saw a couple of others who probably hadn't a lot of spare dollars either.

"Well, I already used proceeds from seized weapons and such to get some jail things."

I saw Old Man Dutton's eyebrows rise up, the way they did, though one of them was interrupted by a scar he had through it now. I nodded at him, 'cause I knew what that eyebrow meant.

"I kept those horses I seized when I started this job on account'a those folks had been warned off when I was a private citizen. But now there are a couple of bushels of guns, and ammo, and half a dozen horses, forfeited in the commission of crimes, and Emilio has gotta be worth twenty dollars a month. All that would pay him for more than a year . . ."

So we decided all of their live horses and their guns and gear and boots would start the jail fund, and I would account for how it got used to the council. Emilio got fifteen dollars a month.

Doc shook his head, and said, "Sheriff Kerrigan, you are more thorough than most highwaymen!" But he had a big grin on when he said it, and the whole room chuckled.

"I appreciate your praise, Doc, but you know," I grinned, looking out the window where those chained miscreants was crouched, shiverin', under Emilio's shotgun, lookin' apprehensive, because he still had bandages showing from under his coat collar, and a lot of scabbing on his scowling face, "this is a *hard* way to fund the law. And I can't really hope for the opportunity to get so much stuff to sell too often."

Doc grinned back."You better *hope* this kind of chance doesn't happen too often, Anse. You had an unbelievable lot of luck this time."

"Well, maybe you should add some more folks to this council, and drop the load all around, make it smaller? Get together everyone and make the council all official, bring anybody who has any kind of business in? Some of the *tienda* owners, the haulers, and so on."

"Anse, you better watch out, or you're likely to wind up being a politician."

Those four started work chained together and they stayed that way, in the cell as well, because I wasn't taking any chances on them jumping Emilio or me when handling them alone. As soon as those broken bones healed some, and their cuts closed, they were chewing jerky and drinking plain water. Doc warned me about something he called "Scurvy," so ever so often we gave the prisoners were with us more than a couple of weeks some *tamarindo* tea, and the occasional bite of apple. You'd think we were handing out whiskey to drunks when we brewed up that tea.

One of the horses we'd seized was a sweet, gentle little appy mare, barely fifteen hands, mostly Spanish Barb. You could take one of her front hooves and put it to her opposite shoulder, she was so flexible. I paid thirty dollars into the jail fund and took her home with me. She made friends with Red and Mule easy. Fact was, they both mooned over her like a couple of lovin' uncles. Gwen took to her like she'd take to a kitten, and I started teaching them both, with good success. Gwen had to wear jeans from the store to get on the saddle, there not being a sidesaddle in all of Las Cruces, and me being of the opinion that those things were ways to hurt a horse's back, anyway. She blushed some the first time she wore them, but she was havin' so much fun she got over her shyness quick.

In any case, Gwen began riding, though it was still cold. She had to wear her own coat, because Miss Eunice would not abide bear smell the way Red had learned to. We kinda expanded our exploration of the area. Gwen had had a pony, when she was young, but this was the first time she'd rode since becomin' a grown woman, and it was fun for all.

Mares tend to change personalities a few times a month, and cowboys are rightfully wary of them, but Miss Eunice and Gwen seemed to be like sisters. Of course, when they changed personalities, I found other things to do.

I did notice that blue jeans totally failed to make Gwen look like a boy. After the first day or two, I noticed those jeans got to fitting better, and Gwen took to leaving her duster home and wearing a short wool jacket. For some reason, the back pockets on those jeans flat vanished the same time they started fitting closer. Red was some puzzled at always riding drag on narrow trails. Gwen seemed awfully happy these days. I was smilin' a lot my ownself.

The town had never looked so good. We had hitching rails, swept walks, raked streets, and soon had three municipal corrals and a well in the town plaza. Those bandits were looking lean and bright-eyed, living so healthy and working so hard. Putting holes in frozen ground was good for, seemed like. And Emilio was enjoying his work. Some of those splinters had left scars, as had the bullet burn, and his smile looked ferocious. He looked like he'd *like* to use his double barreled cannon, and those tough bandits never gave him so much as a cross look.

The average catch of drunks and chicken thieves and so on dropped to almost nothing. That group of four scarred, barefoot, hungry-looking prisoners working somewhere, every day but Sunday, was a real advertisement for law and order.

Still, I got no information about Rogers' hangout or the stores he had.

Gwen's plans and mine were getting along. The new room and porch were almost done, and along about then, Bridget the donkey gave us a little donkey. So much for the fattening nature of *Rio Puerco* grass!

Fact was, everything was going along fine. But I was near out of jail jerky. And I needed some time alone and quiet. So I said my apologies to Gwen, though truth was, she said right off she understood, being as how she wanted to work on some wedding fixings and didn't really want me around just then either. I took Mule and the Duttons' wagon, Red ponied behind, and went north for some elk.

I knew where I wanted to go, but couldn't get the wagon within five miles. So Mule and Red and I came back to our old camp like we'd come before.

There was a bitch wolf livin' in my old lodge, must have been a widow lady, because she hadn't any help for the four tiny cubs I found in there, whilst she fidgeted a hundred yards off, pacin' back and forth, too fearful to come back, too worried about her young 'uns to just leave.

I had meat from a deer I'd taken a couple of days ago, and I put meat in next the cubs, and more in the doorway. That night the moonlight showed her coming back, slinking low, but after the first whimpering of the hungry cubs , there was no more noise, and I fell asleep by my fire, off the other side of my old corral, without seeing her again.

With plenty of ammo for the Henry, and plenty of supplies, taking a few elk and making jerky and leather felt like a vacation. I had plans for those hides, and I worked long and loving on them. I would make a long divided skirt and riding jacket and boots for Gwen from them. Maybe even a new saddle for Miss Eunice.

After a few days of continuing contributions, the lady wolf just moved off a few yards when I brought meat to her den, and sat quiet by the lodge and smiled a sweet doggly smile as we went by on our business, polite-like.

Two weeks' work saw Red and Mule and me packing jerky to the wagon, taking two days to move it all. I had salt, so the jerky was faster than when I'd been making it last year. The carcasses were bigger, too, because in this season the cow elk had calves. I shot the males or barren cows.

I left as big a pile of meat as she could eat in a week for the momma wolf. She watched us go, her young 'uns playing about her. It's always made me feel good to provide for young 'uns. She'd been a quiet neighbor.

The trail down those big hills was still steep even lower than where I had had to leave the wagon, and I spent half my time that day's descent pulling hard on the brake lever, with my heart in my mouth and smoke from the brake block in my nose. Every now and then I had to pour water on it to keep it from bursting into flame. Those travois had been safer.

It was coming on evening; I was about ready to put my beasts to grazing and toast up a steak or two...and the world exploded.

It felt like a torch was being held against my neck, and I was laying on rock, the world spinning.

I rolled, tried to get up, my right leg crumpled, and I hit flat on my face. Pine needles and twigs felt like knives acrost my cheek and eyelid.

So I concentrated on breathing. Seemed like a serious job there for a while. The neck hurt got worse and worse, and then I could sort of fumble with my right arm and leg, and they seemed to be on fire.

I have been shot in the spine. It was a cold, complete thought, and all of a sudden everywhere I could feel was covered in icy fear-sweat.

Looking around is hard when half your body is refusing communication, I want to tell you. It took a while. My wagon, with Red tied to it, was downhill a ways, Mule standing in the traces, patient, Red dancing around, tugging hard on the pony rope that held his halter to the wagon.

All around me was open rock, scattered Ponderosa and Cedar, young stuff. Nowhere to go into cover but over places I couldn't navigate with an arm and a leg not working.

I begun crawling. Red was saddled, with my Henry and Walker riding in their usual places. I felt back of me, found my belt knife. Flopping over, I saw the one Remington I had worn today was still in its holster on my right side.

Seemed like it took forever to get to Red and he got more scared the closer I got. He wasn't used to me flapping around like a fish.

Using the back wagon wheel, I pulled myself up, and hopped around to Red on only my left foot. All of my right side felt on fire, and I think I was moaning some about then. Red steadied down when I got my hand on his neck.

Was no way I could get up on him...and all of a sudden, waiting wasn't an option because I could see horsemen above us, cross-slope, maybe three, four hundred yards off.

I taken out my belt knife and I cut that halter at the cheek piece, talking low to Red, then I sheathed the knife and fell toward the saddle, pulling myself up on the horn to get my feet clear of the ground.

"Git!" Red got. I hung on, my legs thumping and slamming against the scenery, whilst he trotted and ran, going away from the crashing and shouting was coming toward us. A few wild shots whizzed by.

We got maybe a half mile like that, gettin' far enough ahead my pursuers were no longer in eyeshot, 'til Red come up to a stand of mountain mahogany too dense to go through. I wanted desperate to keep him, but hadn't no choice. It was all I could to do to calm him long enough to get the Henry out of the boot. The magazine was full. That would have to do.

Red moved off, skirting the brush, and I said "Git!" again, and he started running. I wished him luck.

I pulled myself into the brush like a broke-back dog. I was hard put not to scream from the burning. I pulled myself in, past roots and sharp rocks, fell over a shelf of granite and hit, rolling. My neck flared up like gunpowder burning, and I was in a fever dream I couldn't get out of for ever so long.

CHAPTER XII

All of a sudden I was awake. It was blackest, freezing night, and the rock I was sprawled across felt like...They used to saw blocks and slabs of ice out of the river, back home, winters, for chilling meat in summer. If you lay against it, it felt like that rock felt. I reached for my face, thoughtless using my right hand, and managed to slap my own eye. Reminded, nose running hard, I let that arm flop down again and tried my right leg. Had some push, *there*!

I tried to sit up, felt cramps knife at my shoulders, felt wetness on my neck.

My left hand told me it was a graze with bone at the bottom, crusted around and maybe two inches long. It went across my neck just below where my skull started and over on the right side, back of my ear, was a bare spot where the bullet had burned off the hair. There was a tender little notch out of the edge of that ear. Thinking back, I realized I had leaned forward to grasp the brake lever just as I was hit. Had I not, my head would have been exploded like a dropped melon.

Maybe just a bruised spine. If so, I would maybe get the use of my hand and arm back. Only not here, and not now. Early spring in the Whites, nights get <u>cold</u>.

I was numb, shaking so hard my teeth were bouncing off each other.

I had to move. I had to get warm or I would die.

The Henry was alongside me, my pistol and knife still with me. Using the Henry, I got up, and managed a shuffle.

It wasn't altogether quiet, but it was moving, and that beat freezing to death on rock.

I looked about for any sign of a fire, because I had no reason to believe my assailants would deny themselves the comfort. I saw nothing. There was a sliver moon, going down now, and it was all I could do to move across that ground without falling. I don't think I made two hundred yards in an hour, but the movement warmed me some. I wore only my elk skin trousers and boots and a shirt so was real glad there was no wind.

I came to a spot where there was a valley of fallen, long-dead trees. Maybe an avalanche or a ground slip had felled them years gone by. I couldn't walk through them, but I could crawl, and I did, for what seemed like an hour.

Deep in a tangle, I nestled between two big trunks and began piling limbs and grasses to make a shelter. It only needed to be six or so feet long, but one-handed, it cost me a miserable time.

Finally, I had a nest; a place where I could lay cushioned on dry stuff and where I had enough cover I might risk a fire. I had matches in a container, made of two cartridge cases, in my belt pouch. Breaking twigs, shaving bark, all took too long, shaking and one-handed, but I kept going, and when I took out a match, I held it between my lips whilst I resealed the rest and got them back in my pouch.

I near smothered that little fire, huddling over it as near as I did, to be sure the first flames were shielded from overhead. Those big downed trees on either side of me made solid walls and I had good barriers either end of my shelter, but wanted to let the fire go to coals before I used its light to finish my roof. By the glowing light of the hand-sized patch of coals, I could see to better my cover, and I did that, fast. That work was helped by having warmed my hands. I was working them together, trying to get feeling back, and rubbing my numb leg. Then I thought some, and reached up and started rubbing my neck. Whatever done it I started to get that arm and leg to moving better.

I wasn't fit, by any means, but I had feeling and some control.

That fire never got to be real big, but it let me survive that night. I was shiverin' for almost an hour before I got warm enough to feel comfortable. Well, as comfortable as someone can be who is almost solid bruise. My neck and particular my right shoulder felt like splintery wood.

In the predawn I piled dirt on the fire. I didn't want any smoke coming up in the daylight to show my position.

I was surely regretting those steaks I hadn't had last night. Just a year back, I had gone days and weeks on little or no food. Now I missed one meal and felt deprived. Shows you how a man can get spoiled, hanging around women and all. I tell you true, what I wanted most along about then was to go back to being spoiled!

I could not get out of those mountains without a horse. But the people who had shot me had probably caught Red. So my first job was to locate my enemies because it was likely they had the only horses up here. And then I thought hard and realized that I not only owed it to Mule to see what had happened to him, because I had left him harnessed in the traces of a wagon and he deserved better, but I had *learned* to ride on him!

So instead of going up the way Red had gone, I made my way down-mountain, keeping in the brush and moving just a bit at a time. I came to the last cover just before the open area of widely spaced young trees where I had been ambushed and I could see that I did not need to go out in the open.

Mule sprawled in the traces, held propped up by the harness they had not bothered to cut when they had shot him.

Mule had been Ma's, and I had learned to ride on his back before I could walk. I had grown up eating food grown from fields he had pulled the plow through; he had carried my possessions across a cold and hostile country. I had balked at the idea of hanging men that had tried to kill *me*. But killing a sweet, simple animal was worse, somehow. I made up my mind, crouched there, that those men were going to die.

That wagon, and poor mule, were not exact where they had been when Red and I escaped. They were on a little spot was almost level, and crosswise of the way we had been going. Both a wagon and a mule are valuable things, and the thousand or so pounds of jerky and the hides on board were too. It held food and equipment, ammunition, blankets, or it had; I dared not go anywhere near it. They had shot Mule to make that wagon a bait, to draw me in for killing.

I determined that since I could not move quietly and they were sure to be close by I was better off holding still because I might be able to out-wait them.

It was a long morning. Changing position was painful, and probably dangerous. It was odd how good the sun had felt when it first struck me...and how much it hurt after a couple of hours. I was touchy and sore all over. And, of course, I had lost my good Texas hat when I was shot. Used to wearing it outdoors, an' mostly being indoors for months, I sunburned up pretty good in that fine sunshine coming through thin mountain air.

My neck and shoulders ached fierce, more so as the sunshine loosened them up some. It was exact like I'd been beaten...or shot. Inside of my mouth was dry, and it was gettin' hard to swallow. My seeing got blurry ever so often, and had a way of going double, and my skull felt like it was gonna pop.

About noon, I caught a glint of light, off a mile or so, acrost a canyon. I started thinking, fast!

Here I'd been figuring they'd be waiting in rifle range, to ambush me. That meant no more than a hundred fifty yards for the usual saddle guns, but then one of them had a buffalo gun or the like, since I'd been shot from at least five hundred yards.

If they had binoculars, or a telescope, I could be spotted from a couple of miles, maybe. Me being afoot, they could maneuver and close on me from a long way out.

I'd never owned any such thing myself, and it wasn't something that came quick to mind. Now, though, I sank down still more in the brush, getting as low as I could.

If they were glassing for me, judging from where that glint come from, up a little rocky peak where a horse couldn't go, whoever was there doing the glassing wasn't expected to get to the wagon fast and easy. That meant others, set so a signal would alert them. If their lookout spotted me, I could be charged right off.

Now my Henry was the .44-40, and was good out to five or six hundred yards, and still further in the hands of a really good distance shot. And while I had done some practicing this past year, the shape I was in I didn't fancy shooting further than I had to. The Henry's magazine holding thirteen rounds was nice; but that was all the rifle ammo I had, and my right hand bein' shaky meant my trigger pull and my aim would be off. I couldn't expect to fight them at a distance. I had to hold still and hope.

That long morning turned into a long day. When night was come, I taken a big chance. I moved out on that slope, taking it easy and slow; headed for that wagon. They'd no reason to have taken my canteens, and I'd had a keg of water aboard too, for the animals. Nearest water I could recall, havin' been through this area a few times now, was a couple of miles away. Wasn't sure I could make it that far. And it was gettin' cold again.

Only a cough saved me. Sounded like a man who used tobacco, muffled and desperate low. It came again, still lower, like the man was holding his hand hard on his mouth, or smothering the cough in a coat.

He's in the wagon!

Hindsight made it obvious that having a man in the wagon was good tactics. Maybe I wasn't thinking too clear, neck shot, and tired and hungry and thirsty and all.

So they had a man in the wagon. And there had been a watcher over acrost the canyon earlier. So where were the others? I had glimpsed at least three, yesterday. There were probably four left in that Rogers gang...and why anyone else would ambush me was a question.

On the one hand, I had an enemy located. That was an advantage. On the other hand was the problem of noise. If I shot him, I would quickly be outnumbered, and I had no horse and could not run on my own bad leg.

Those elk skin boots and trousers were quiet. I moved to the wagon crouched low, though I wobbled some, and had to use my hand as a crutch, often enough. Using every bit of cover I could, I aimed to come up behind the tailgate. That was solid, and a bit higher than the sides.

When I got there, I put the Henry down slow and quiet, taking pains not to breathe heavy, scuff dirt, nor nothing else made noise. Then I went back to waiting. I was getting some tired of waiting, I tell you true.

The fellow coughed again, and again he muffled it, but now I knew just where he was; in behind the driver's seat.

If I touched that wooden wagon, he would know it. So I couldn't climb up. But being as how he had to have been in place all day, he had to be needing to move; he sure wanted a stretch, or to relieve himself.

Sure enough, after I had held still for what seemed like hours, I heard him coming out. The moon wasn't up yet, though this night it would be tiny. I was some grateful for the dark, though I was beginning to shiver again, holding still like that. He climbed down, clumsy, like a man had been in one place all day; when he put his gun belt down real careful, scuffed a cathole with the heel of his boot, and I could hear him loose his belt, I knew why.

He was hunkered there by the outside of the left front wheel, and I was seven, eight feet away, under the wagon body. I unsheathed my knife, taking a long time, because of using my left hand that wasn't so sure as my right usually was.

When he straightened from his business, he would adjust his clothing before he reached down for his gun belt. That would be the moment he was farthest from his weapons.

I got to him in one long stumble, and just as my damned leg went useless, put the point into his kidney. I bore down on the haft hard, to brace myself up. He gasped, but before he could come out with a scream, I flung my right hand around, covering his mouth, pulled him back and down hard and fast, falling over myself. I was pent up from a long, worrisome day, and I think I broke his back. I cut his throat clear to bone all the way acrost anyway.

That made some noise, of course, bubbling and spraying sounds, mainly. So I held still and listened some more. Actually, I *had* to hold still, because my right arm and shoulder felt like I'd torn them up, yankin' loose deep cramps.

Cut the way he'd been, he'd sprayed forward, but my left hand and knife had some blood on them, and I took pains to use his shirt to clean them. He hadn't been washin' too often, and I promised myself to boil some water to clean my knife soon as I could. Was kind of fragrant, with his cat hole part covered, and his having had more inside that came out when he died, and all. I kicked a lot of loose soil to absorb the worst of it. Killin' is a messy business.

He had a pistol and a knife on the gun belt, and in the wagon he had a shotgun, a double-barreled one, felt like a breach loader. Feeling around I found a belt of shells for that, and *my* blankets he had been using, and some other needfuls.

Water, a lot of water, a couple of hard biscuits, and a gnaw of jerky had me feeling some better. My spare boxes and bandolier of Henry ammo were in the tool box under the seat, where I had left them; I put together a canteen, food, ammo, made a sling pack with thongs out of the blankets and my soogan. I put a box of matches in, and dug out my other Remington and spare cylinders, too.

I was going to take that shotgun, and the Henry and the bandolier. That was a lot of weight, but I needed it all.

When I had done kitting up in the dark, the little sliver moon was up, and again I stayed put for fear of detection. If any of them were close enough to make out the body on the ground, I had the shotgun and the concealment of the wagon.

I ate slowly and steadily while I waited for moonfall. I had biscuits, jerky, and some dried apples, and my other canteen was still full. I got to feeling positively comfortable, and then I looked out of the wagon and saw Mule laying there dead in the cool moonlight. I wasn't cheerful no more.

When you go hunting you better not hunt something can hunt back. I figured those fellas had made just that mistake, this time.

Daylight found me flat alongside a lightning-killed spruce that lay across the brow of one of them canyons. I was a thousand feet above the wagon and half of a mile distant. That was as far as I'd been able to get between moonfall and predawn, and it had been a steep scramble. I hadn't binoculars, but had good night eyes.

Not long after sunrise, a rider with a ponied horse come out of the timber below the wagon, and he was near to it before his mount started bucketing and wheeling from the blood and other smells. The ponied animal joined the dance, stirrups flappin' and slappin', which made it wilder, and it tore loose of the rider's grip. He hadn't done the dumb thing I see sometimes, tying the pony string to a saddle ring, but he flipped his hand like he'd got a good rope burn. The led horse probably belonged to the waylayer I'd killed, and bore *his* saddle and bridle. No one likes adjustin' tack once he's got it right for himself. Well, that was one worry that fella hadn't no more.

That rider dismounted, like a sensible man, and led his horse on in, his pistol in hand. I couldn't make out his face from my distance, but he was considerable bigger than Rogers. He turned and shouted back at the timber he had come out of. *Three* other riders came a'smokin'.

They all dismounted; two of them cast out, looking for sign. But my boots had thick, soft pads of elk skin for soles, and no sharp edges. They were really like heavy moccasins. So it was going to be some difficult to track me over that hard ground and rock.

Still, they found some sign, because they all came on the route I'd taken up hill. They passed from my sight in a fold of the mountain, and I waited.

Over the canyon brow just behind me was a deer trail went down into boulders about two hundred yards below, where I had cached my food and water and that shotgun and one of my pistols. There weren't nothing but a couple of ponderosas within hundreds of feet in front of my downed spruce, so I had me a clear killing field and a safe line of retreat. I had listened some to the veterans come home from the war.

I set up the rear ladder sight of the Henry and waited, and pretty soon they showed, riding slow, with two out ahead tracking careful. It was difficult ground for horses in places, but I hadn't been able to go through some of the worst places myself, with my injury, and so they had it easier than I would have liked.

Range was maybe two hundred and fifty yards. I waited some more.

When the range was down to about one fifty, extreme range for their saddle guns and way out of range for their pistols, I sighted on the farthest one back, and squeezed off real careful. Then I worked that lever for all I was worth, and put a lot of lead into that bunch as they milled and hopped around. A couple of them fell off their horses, though I couldn't know if they were hit. The one I had shot careful for was down and still.

I kept one eye 'round the end of that spruce trunk whilst I put some more cartridges into the Henry. I'd plenty in the bandolier, but the Henry was squeasin' dry. Wasn't a movin' man in sight. But two horses was bawling and screaming ...and another man was down! I saw him as he flopped over and made to crawl ahint a rock; I shot him, through the chest, because I saw dust jump off his vest. He didn't move no more.

Then bark and chips were coming off my log, and ricochets were screaming around all indiscriminate. I made my retreat into that canyon, crawling over the rim spry as could be, keeping that spruce between me and those shooters. That stone up there is sharp and altogether too common, and a good part of my shirt failed to escape with me.

The sound of rock-flattened lead slobbering around is one of the best motivators to motion I know of.

It was a steep down, and I fell and rolled a couple of times, takin' off skin I'd just as soon have kept, but I kept hold of the Henry. My handgun was thonged in, like always. I had to hop and lurch and stumble, but I did the *fastest* hop, lurch, and stumble you can imagine.

The boulders were solid cover, and now I had my persecutors needing to come over the lip of the canyon, skylined, with the sun behind them. And of course I had my firing spot already set up, so *I* only had the muzzle of my rifle and one eye showin', and those in shadow.

I waited some more, hoping they were dumb enough or mad enough to come direct after me. But when they came, they came over the rim up and down canyon of me, and they came over fast, moving to cover.

These were trained and experienced fighting men. Despite having some recent experience and luck, I hadn't anything like the war experience such men had.

The man was up-canyon of me started firing, putting rounds into cover, obvious searching, probing.

Should I fire, the one down-canyon would have me in a cross fire, because they had guessed right; splitting up as they had, I was bracketed.

I held still and stayed down, though he put some lead around my pet boulders.

After a while, the other one took up firing. I was getting good at holding still so I stuck with that.

It seemed to work. After a long while, they both scrambled back over the rim.

But I was suspicious. Sure enough, after maybe ten minutes, both of them jumped over the rim, in new places, took cover, and looked real intent over their sights.

They were hoping to catch me moving.

One, looked to be Rogers himself, finally stood and waved t'other one back, and both scrambled up to the canyon edge again, only Roger's toady went over and out of sight *just* before Rogers did. So I firmed my aim, already on him, and squeezed careful, but Rogers didn't drop from a heart shot as I'd intended. Instead he yelled, clutched the calf of his right leg. Then he was over the rim, leavin' just a spatter of blood on a grey rock, bright lit by the sun.

My shaky hand had failed me and I was deep disappointed. I still had two opponents, it was broad daylight, and I simply was stuck. Add to that, while they had been firing saddle guns just then, they had a long range rifle either close by or available back where I'd ambushed 'em. I couldn't just retreat to get out of range, because the rims of the little canyon I'd homesteaded were only about four hundred yards apart, firing straight from one to t'other, and there wasn't any real cover near the other rim. Moving up or down canyon wasn't going to move me out of range of that hostile rim near fast enough.

I stayed quiet. Neither one had seen me fire, and while they knew now I was still in range, they didn't know exactly where I was.

Couldn't see either of them, though I was sure they was hunkered down and sightin' this area. Rogers had moved too spry to count him out. I wasn't feeling any too spry my ownself, havin' added considerable to my collection of bruises and scrapes gettin' here.

They stayed missing. But mindful of their distance glass and buffalo gun, I waited amongst those boulders through that long sunburned day, frequent looking about to see was I being flanked. At nightfall I moved across my hiding canyon and circled back around its top end. I moved slow and quiet, taking a long time to listen real frequent.

Now I had been awake for two days and a night, and the night before that had not been restful. So I crept into a thicket was deep enough to give warning should I be approached and I wrapped up in my blankets and soogan and went to sleep.

My own hydraulic system woke me before dawn. After I peered around for close-by company, I taken just long enough to rub my face with water from the canteen and to munch some biscuit and dried apples. I used a corner of a blanket to wipe the dew off my weapons and made up my pack. One other chore; I tied a bit of my shirt tail on a thong, and put the thong down the bore of the Henry with a bit of lead cut from one of my remington slugs clamped about it. Should have used boiling water and a brush, but a few passes with that patch cleaned most of the buildup out of the rifling.

Coming out of cover, I decided to look around where I had dropped those men.

The bodies were there, and off a ways was a dead horse, too. I was some anxious, but it wasn't Red. All the dead men's weapons and gear were gone, but those bandits hadn't even put a coat across their friends' faces, and the ravens already had the eyes and tongues, the way they do. An early morning couple of them took off as I come up, and I froze for a while, fearful I had sent up a signal.

Vernon had been the one I had dropped first; I didn't know the other one.

I didn't want to track direct. These dead folks had just been shown how dangerous that could be.

Anticipating the gang's movement was going to be hard. Water was frequent, so I couldn't predict their travel by watering holes, the way you could down in the dry country. To add to the difficulty, I didn't know how or where they were based, or if they had more men somewhere.

Still, they had gone a long way beyond what I could forgive, even was I inclined to.

I decided to go downhill a couple miles and work across-slope. If I didn't cut their trail today, I would tomorrow or the next day.

CHAPTER XIII

My hand kept going numb and then tingling and so did parts of my right leg. A couple of times that leg went out from under me without any warning. One of those times I hit ground hard enough to hurt bad. Still, I kept a pretty steady pace for a fellow who was inclined to hug trees and rocks and anything else looked like cover. Every time I crossed open ground, I felt like a mouse in a mowed meadow.

I had that shotgun thonged to my pack, and the Henry and Remingtons weren't light, neither. Being without a horse sure changes your thinking about what to take along on a picnic.

Still, hunting at least two men, I wanted every piece of ironmongery I had. If I had come across a piece of field artillery I would have been downright reluctant to leave it behind, right then.

Along about noon I heard shouted cursing, and I figured I might have found my men, because the language was awful...and in Rogers' East Texas accent.

"Yu cut that Gawuddayamned thang any deepah and Aih'll hev yore...... !"

Well, you probably get the idea.

Sounded like Rogers was enjoying some surgery.

And they weren't worried I might hear them.

I figured they must think I was running *away* from them. My having gone deeper, or rather, higher, into the mountains after I got some gear and food might have fooled them.

After all, how many folks would elect to go into a fight of four or five to one?

Thing is, they probably hadn't realized what shooting Mule had done to their prospects, and now there were only two of them left. I *hoped* there were only two of them left.

They were in a clump of high-growing *piñon* that screened them from my view.

One thing I had learned hunting was that it was safer to move if something was looking away from you than if it was looking in your direction. Since I couldn't see them, I couldn't know where they were looking at any given time, but that meant they probably couldn't see me, neither. Odds were it was safe to move.

I was really tired of waiting, in any case. My face was all raw peeling hurt, my lips cracked, I had bruises everywhere, and it seemed my right side was getting worse. So I bellied down and circled to have cover coming up on that clump of trees.

My shirt was altogether gone at the elbows from all this crawling around; something else I was getting real tired of. Truth to tell, I was getting serious *mad.*

Mountain mahogany and some bunch grass gave me concealment until I was maybe forty yards out from the edge of that grove, and I hadn't heard anything since Rogers had done that bellowing.

I saw movement, screened not only by the trees, but by the grasses and bushes I was down amongst. I almost pulled trigger on the Henry, but realized in time I was seeing a horse, moving restless like it was on a tie line and unhappy with flies.

Their horses could be more danger to me than they were. Fortunate, the wind was quartering away from them and toward me.

I still had that pack and shotgun slung, because I had no idea where I would have to go, once the party started.

I got myself into the *piñon* clump proper and eased upright behind one of them. It wasn't thick and solid and bullet proof and comforting like a ponderosa. And while it *was* concealment, fact was, I couldn't get in anywhere near the trunk in any case, because *piñons* bush out most like one of those junipers. And they have got all manner of dead stuff down around them.

That right leg gave way on me without any warning; just wasn't there for a second, and then it was, but in recovering I had stomped twigs loud enough to wake the dead.

In the instant it took me to regain my balance, bullets blasted all around me. I felt a burn across my chest, my bandolier yanked, spun me around like a top, and I fell flat, skidding.

They were coming fast; I heard boots thumping toward me, though I still couldn't see anything. I rolled, and that shotgun caught a root or something, and stopped me cold. Bullets blasted leaf duff and rock chips where I would have rolled *to*, but I didn't have time to be grateful to providence just then.

Frantic, I wrestled out of the pack thong, shedding shotgun and all, trying to keep hold of the Henry. They were on me, Rogers and that big man I'd never seen close before. Rogers was levering in a fresh cylinder, and the other fellow was holstering one handgun and yankin' another from behind his back. Rogers had his gunbelt slung acrost his chest, was barefoot, had no trousers on, and the right leg of his long johns had been cut away up to the knee. He had blood all over that calf and foot, and he hitched bad as he strode at me. I got to my left knee and just looking along the barrel, not sighting, though I did get the butt into my shoulder, levered that rifle so fast it emptied in one swing acrost my front. Gun smoke made a cloud in front of me that was almost solid. My right leg lurched again, hard, and as I swung around, falling, I saw the gash from knee to hip, where a bullet had ripped. The smoke blew away in grey tatters.

"Yu dog-kissin' shike-poke! Aih'm gohn shute yure Gawudayamed aihs ayout!"

Rogers looked so mad I almost expected him to froth at the mouth, but though he was obvious screaming I could barely hear him. He was levering another cylinder into his Remington. I couldn't see the other man, but that gun smoke was like a moving curtain still.

I lurched to sit up, drawing both my own Remingtons, only the right one fell out of my hand before I could raise it, and the hand was so numb I just *saw* the hog leg fall, couldn't feel it.

I got the other pistol going though, and I saw Rogers' revolver blow smoke and flame toward me. I wasn't hearing anything just then.

I was up on my knees, shooting as careful as I could, and then Rogers turned and stumbled away.

It taken me a couple tries to get to my feet, and I was reeling, but I followed him as he staggered back through the *piñons*. Where that other fellow had gone, I did not know, but I was going to get this one killed proper. He stumbled out into a little clearing where four horses were on a tie line, rearing and bucking from all the noise.

Bad off as I was, I saw one of them was Red! He even had my saddle still on him.

Rogers was turning to face me, and I saw what I had done to him and a probable reason his aim was not good.

He had only the top half of his face and a little bit of the lower jaw on his left side. If he'd had a mouth left, I bet he'd have been cussing. What was left of his tongue was flappin' about, anyway, flecked with shattered bits of teeth.

I was shocked. I'd been shooting for where he was biggest.

I brought my weapon to bear, but it clicked empty when I went to fire. Rogers' pistol was wavering around and then he got it trained on my face, and *his* went off as I threw myself down and forward. Though the round missed my face, I felt it put *another* notch in my poor abused right ear, and felt powder particles sting my cheek. He hung his head forwards, squinted under his eyebrows, hammered back, pulled trigger again, and clicked empty. He looked at his pistol and at me, and dropped it. I remembered to breathe.

I reached for a cylinder, only to realize that I couldn't shift hands to hold the Remington while I exchanged the cylinders.

Keeping my eyes locked on Rogers, I stumbled over to where Red was snorting and tugging on his lead, crooning to him. I think I was crooning; couldn't hear a thing.

He let me stroke his neck, rolling his eyes and throwing his head. I petted him, and pretty quick he was still. All that time I kept my eyes on Rogers. He just stood there, shaking, front of his shirt solid red now. *Where was that other man?*

The Walker was in its flapped holster at the front of my saddle. It was about all I could to do get it out and cocked. Rogers was looking straight into my eyes. With the big pistol held between *his* eyes, I walked all wobbly over to him, kicked and tossed his guns and knife away, so he couldn't be reloading or doing any other mischief while my back was to him, then I went careful back to Red.

Rogers sagged to his knees.

I kneeled my ownself, and holding my Remington's barrel firm against the ground with my knee, leaning against

Red's foreleg, I got it recylindered and reholstered one handed. Rearmed, I went, cautious, to search for t'other Mule killer.

There he was, tangled deep in the debris under a *piñon*, and he was most certainly dead, with two from the Henry having gone in his shirt pockets, so to speak. Holes in his back were the size of my fists. Looking closer, I saw where a bandana he had tied around his neck was all bloody. I pulled it down and saw a raw bullet gouge was a day or so old. It had taken me two tries on this one too.

I shoved the Walker in my waistband and recovered my right hand pistol, pack, and unlimbered that shotgun I'd been toting. A scattergun seemed appropriate to my condition, because I was not really sure where I was pointed.

Rogers had not moved out of his kneel and he never took his eyes off me as I gathered all their weapons and put them on those other horses and holstered the Walker and Henry back on Red's saddle. I got a headstall and reins from a pile of them, and bridled Red, right over the halter he was wearing, taking what seemed like forever, and about the time I got done with that, I saw tears come out to join the blood as Rogers swayed there.

He just kneeled there and trembled, the shock wearing off and the pain taking him while I cut up a blanket and bound a pad on my ear, wrapped my torn leg. The bullet burn across my chest was hurting but not serious.

My hearing was back good enough to hear him moaning and bubbling. He was still kneeling there when I reined away with that shotgun acrost my saddlebow. Mule had been my friend.

It was a strangled, burblin' sort of scream stopped me. He had his hands up to me, like he was praying. It was a hard choice, I tell you true, but I'd have to tell Gwen what happened.

When I done him the kindness, the shotgun took off a lot more of his head. I left him laying there for the ravens, and rode down the big hills.

EPILOGUE

Doc found a bit of fractured bone was pressing on my spinal cord, shifting some when I moved. It hadn't cut in, and soon as he tweezered it out, my right side cleared up. I still get a stiff neck when the weather changes, though.

Now you will have to excuse me, but Gwen will have supper ready...and I do hate to miss one of her meals.

Sutton
Big Hills
112

David Lloyd Sutton

The author is son of a father who was a mule skinner and small town constable and a mother who was born in a sod-fronted dugout. She actually arrived in California via Conestoga wagon.

David learned the old western skills and ethos by assimilation, spending his first eleven years living in a tent, neighbored by deer, coyotes, and bobcats, helping to raise the family's food, and employing many of the techniques he has used in this book. From the age of twelve, he was spending all his free time, often gained by playing hooky, living off his rifle in the wild country inland of Santa Barbara, his birthplace. He is still most at home in wilderness.

Volunteering into the Marine Corps at seventeen, he served two (also voluntary) combat tours in Vietnam, leaving the service as a sergeant. "I was a bloodthirsty child" he says. Since then he has captained an abalone boat, tested lightning arresters, and was the Gadget Skunk Works for Hughes' infrared research facility for a decade.

In the then-New Hebrides, working for the *real* Phoenix Foundation, he wrote a constitution for their independence movement whilst training militia officers and running a police force. The socialists won, and he's on the proscribed persons list in that place now.

Possessed of black belts in Karate and Kobudo, a long time NRA instructor, he has some authority in his fighting-action writing.

Amusingly, science fiction is his first literary love, and he has one completed novel in that genre being marketed and another just entering the launch bay.

David has moved into full novel work from a long history of short stories and fact articles, largely in equestrian, martial arts, and firearms magazines. He says, "Every technique in this book is real, and I've either done it or seen it done."

The author's experience set goes a long way toward explaining the immediacy and clarity of this read. Also some of its humor. He adds, "I've come hard off a big chestnut just as often as my character."

www.ingramcontent.com/pod-product-compliance
Lightning Source LLC
Chambersburg PA
CBHW071324130626
46556CB00004B/1734